The Gor Incident

Veslor Mates – Book One

By Laurann Dohner

The Gorison Traveler Incident

by Laurann Dohner

Vivian is a cultural specialist on the United Earth fleet ship *Gorison Traveler*. It's the perfect job for someone who wants to learn everything about aliens. The only problem? The commander won't let her anywhere near the visiting Ke'ters aboard the ship. The only way she gets a peek at the lizard-like race is when her brother opens a live camera feed during a meeting—a meeting that turns tragic when the Ke'ters attack the crew.

She's horrified. Scared. The Ke'ters are murdering her people. Rushing from her quarters to get help from a control center, Vivian finds the station abandoned. It's all on her to try to rescue the crew.

Brassi is a Veslor trader who picks up a distress signal from a nearby space vessel. The attractive female who contacts him looks terrified, and needs his help. He'll board the *Gorison Traveler* with his crewmates, and fight the Ke'ters, but the longer he spends on the huge Earth vessel, the greater

2

distraction Vivian becomes. Brassi will do whatever it takes to save her…and to discover if Vivian's his mate.

Veslor Mates Series List

The Gorison Traveler Incident

The Gorison Traveler Incident by Laurann Dohner

Editor: Kelli Collins

Cover Art: Dar Albert

ISBN: 978-1-950597-01-7

Chapter One   6

Chapter Two   21

Chapter Three   39

Chapter Four   53

Chapter Five   67

Chapter Six   80

Chapter Seven   95

Chapter Eight   108

Chapter Nine   126

Chapter Ten   136

Chapter Eleven   148

Chapter Twelve   162

Chapter Thirteen   177

Chapter Fourteen   191

Epilogue   203

The Gorison Traveler Incident

Veslor Mates – Book One

By Laurann Dohner

Chapter One

Vivian grinned, staring at Mikey over the vid device. "You know this is going to be the most boring meeting ever."

"You should come join me."

"No, thank you. I've had to sit through too many of those security team leader meetings. That's why I became a cultural specialist."

"Dad wouldn't have kept you with him at all times as a teenager if you hadn't gotten into so much trouble."

She laughed. "True enough. Aren't you glad I'm all grown up now?"

"I'm just glad you're back home where you belong. We missed you while you were gone."

She'd missed her adopted brother and father, too. She'd been thrilled when she'd finished her schooling and gotten hired to work with them on the *Gorison Traveler*, as her first official job.

He shifted in his seat. "Dad's on his way."

"Tell Big M hello for me when you get a chance. I guess it's time to end our conversation."

Mikey flashed her a mischievous look. "You don't want to see what the Ke'ters look like? Dad sent a notice that a small group of them were joining us. He didn't want anyone to be alarmed at the sight of them."

Excitement suddenly had her heart racing. "Why are they at a team leader debriefing?"

He shrugged. "Maybe they're curious to find out how we keep everyone safe, or how we run things on a vessel this large? Who knows. But they're here." He turned his handheld vid device enough for her to get a view of the large room. Dozens of men and women in security uniforms were seated in rows in front of him, and she saw her adopted father walk into the room with six large aliens.

A delegation for the Ke'ters had boarded the *Gorison Traveler* at the Branston Space Station ten days earlier. Vivian's duties included profiling and interacting with alien races, but Commander Alderson had banned her from going anywhere near their important guests. It hadn't surprised her. She was new to the job, had breasts, and he held a grudge that her family association to Big M, the ship's head of security, had procured her the job.

She still fumed that she had been ordered to stay far away from their alien guests. The Ke'ters were a mostly unknown race, currently trying to gain an alliance with United Earth. It would have been an amazing opportunity to study them and share whatever she'd learned with her fellow cultural specialists.

The Ke'ters had approached Commander Alderson on the space station after being introduced by the station director, a friend of his, who'd vouched for their trustworthiness. Vivian guessed the real reason

8

the commander had agreed was to score points with the higher-ups. He could gain a huge promotion if he talked the Ke'ters into giving up some of their technology. Rumor had it they were advanced in weaponry.

Mikey lowered his voice, whispering, "They're big...and they kind of remind me of Pete."

She shushed him. Pete was Mikey's pet iguana. She silently agreed, though. The Ke'ters were a reptilian race with thick arms and legs. They walked upright, but were lizard-like otherwise. Black claws dominated the ends of their three long fingers and one thumb-like hooked appendage that came out of what would be the palm area of their hands, if they'd been human. The Ke'ters also had wide heads attached to slim, long necks. Their uniforms covered most of their skin, but the exposed scales appeared dense.

"Everyone, quiet down." Big M took the podium, the room going silent. "I'd like to introduce you to Krrnt Sheesk. He's the ambassador we're hosting, and he'd like to say a few words."

Vivian appreciated that Mikey kept their link open, the camera focused on the aliens. It was the only way she'd get to see them while they were aboard. One of them stepped closer to Big M. Her adopted father was tall for a human, but the alien next to him stood taller, putting him around six and a half feet.

"We are grateful you let us on your ship." The translator device strapped around Krrnt Sheesk's throat provided a robotic male voice. Their natural language was just clicks and hisses to human ears. "And now we will show our appreciation." He paused, turning his head to glance at the others in his group. "Humans are a naive race—but tasty."

Vivian gasped when the aliens suddenly lunged forward, aiming for the rows of security officers.

But her focus remained on Krrnt Sheesk as he grabbed ahold of Big M and threw him hard at the wall.

Mikey cursed, the vid device moving fast enough that the reception on it blurred. She got flashes of laser blasts hitting the Ke'ters but they didn't fall or slow their attacks. It was clear the weapons couldn't pierce their scales. Damage occurred to their uniforms only.

Mikey backed up, his weapon still firing.

"Vivian, alert the commander!"

She was too shocked to respond, still watching as the aliens leapt on security officers, taking them to the floor and ripping open their bellies.

More screams and shouting. The laser fire almost drowning his next words.

"Dad! They killed Dad!"

She shoved out of her chair and rushed to the wall panel next to her door, hitting the button for security.

A calm male voice answered. "What is your emergency?"

"The Ke'ters are attacking everyone at the team leader debriefing. They're killing them!"

"*What?*"

"I'm watching it! Big M is dead! Oh my god. Send security! Help them. The Ke'ters are murdering everyone!"

"This better not be a joke." He sounded upset though, his voice raising to almost a shout.

"Help them!"

He ended the call, and she rushed back to her desk where her vid device sat. Mikey had retreated to the back of the room, still firing on the aliens.

"Help is coming. Hang on, Mikey!"

He turned his vid device, and Vivien stared into his shocked eyes. "Get to Control One. Lock in," he ordered. His gaze left hers—then terror flashed across his face.

Something hit him and the vid device went flying. It landed on the floor.

All she could see was the ceiling…but she heard screams, shouting, and more laser fire.

Forever seemed to pass but it had to be less than a minute in reality. It grew eerily quiet, with only some low moans and hissing sounds.

Was Mikey alive?

She sat there in stunned silence, afraid to say a word. They'd hear her if they were close enough to the open vid device. Ke'ters had excellent hearing. It was one of the few known facts about them.

"We take the ship," a robotic voice stated, soft, but she was able to hear it. "We will bring our planet plenty of food."

Horror seeped into her bones, making Vivian feel ice-cold.

They were talking about people. Krrnt Sheesk had said humans were tasty. There were six hundred and twenty-three humans aboard the ship.

Vivian reached out, ended the connection and ran for the wall safe. Big M had given her a laser rifle. He'd also taught her self-defense and various fighting methods in the hopes she'd one day become a security officer.

The rifle wouldn't do her much good. She'd seen how ineffective lasers had been on the aliens. But she removed her dad's tactical blade and belt. Big M had presented them to her at the funeral of his best friend, her father. She'd never used it, but Big M had trained her with knives, too.

She walked to the door, strapping on the too-large belt to sheathe the blade, and flipped on the monitor that showed the corridor beyond. No one waited outside and no other crew members were in sight.

She gripped the handle of the blade and opened the door, stepping out.

Control One was four decks up and on the other side of the ship.

Her heart pounded as she made her way to the lift and pushed to call it to her deck. She backed up, prepared to fight when the doors opened. Fear had her glancing around as she went over what she knew about the Ke'ters.

Twenty-two of them had boarded in total. Eight were security officers, meaning they'd be good fighters. All of them were male, from what Big M had told her over dinner after they'd arrived. Meat-eaters.

She winced. "Including humans," she whispered.

The lift opened, blessedly empty of life. She rushed inside and hit the button. The doors sealed and she backed into a corner, keeping a firm grip on the knife handle. She only hoped she wouldn't have to use it—and if she did, that it was sharp enough to pierce scales.

The doors opened on Deck Seven and she inched forward, not hearing any sounds of fighting. The alarms on the ship hadn't gone off, either. That confused her. They were under attack. Security should have done that much, at least. It was procedure.

She walked down the corridor—and froze when she heard someone scream.

Vivien threw herself against the wall, turning her head in the direction of the sound. The corridor curved up ahead and whatever was happening, it was close. She slid forward, pulling the long blade out of her belt.

The scream cut off, and seconds later she heard loud moaning. A hiss sounded, and she held her breath, peeking around the corner.

The sight that met her gaze almost made *her* scream.

A Ke'ter was crouched over someone in a white medical uniform that was stained red. Their stomach had been torn open, their intestines ripped out and piled on the deck floor. The alien leaned in close to its victim—and Vivian heard wet smacking sounds.

The alien was eating the crew member.

She saw the victim turn his head. He was still alive!

Her horror grew when their gazes met and his mouth opened. Another moan came from him, and he lifted his hand, reaching toward her.

The alien kept chewing, but he might notice his victim's actions at any moment.

She had no time to think. Big M and Mikey had trained her to defend herself.

She lunged around the corner and jumped on the Ke'ter's back.

He was solidly built, like hitting rock, but she hooked her left arm around his throat and squeezed hard with her thighs around his middle. Using all her strength, she rammed the knife into the back of his head near the base of his skull.

The blade penetrated and the alien under her screeched.

He tried to fling her off, but she pushed the blade in deeper and twisted.

He stilled...and then slumped.

Vivien scrambled off him when they hit the floor. The poor crew member stared at her when she looked at him, his mouth still open, eyes wide, and another moan sounded.

She crouched next to the man. He wasn't someone she knew. "Hold on," she told him. "I'm getting help." She tore her gaze from his and looked down at his stomach.

Bile rose. The Ke'ter had torn the man open from the bottom of his rib cage to his pelvis, shredding his uniform and skin open a good ten inches. She was no doctor, but it looked as if the alien had pulled out the man's intestines to feed on his internal organs. It was a gory mess.

A low hiss came from the alien, and she almost fell on her ass in startled surprise. The Ke'ter's hand twitched, the bloody claws and fingers curling.

She lunged at it, going for the weapon strapped to its hip, and jerked it out of the holster. It felt strange in her hand, the grip weird since it hadn't been designed for humans, but there was a button. She pointed the muzzle at the alien and pushed it.

It blew a hole in the Ke'ter's uniform and green blood oozed out onto the floor.

She rose up, pointed at its head, and fired again.

The alien jerked, but she doubted it was still alive. A fist-sized hole had blasted through its skull.

She walked closer and used her left hand to grab her father's tactical knife. It wouldn't come free of the alien's head. She released it when the crew member moaned again in pain. She turned her head to look at him.

"I'm getting help. Hold on."

She ran toward Control One. It was manned twenty-four/seven by operators who worked in single-person shifts. She knew the ship's protocols better than most security officers.

The doors were sealed. She buzzed but no one answered.

Fear had her staring up at the camera. "Open up, damn it!"

The doors remained sealed.

A faint scream sounded from somewhere down one of the corridors, and she quickly used her left hand to type in the override code. She wasn't supposed to know it, but Big Mike had entrusted her with the numbers.

The doors slid open—but the desk sat empty.

Shock slapped her again. *No one* should have left that post unattended. It was against ship protocol.

She entered, the doors sealing at her back.

She put the alien weapon on the desk as she slid into the seat, her fingers quickly manipulating the controls to pull up the debriefing room.

The sight that met her gaze made her cry out in grief.

Mikey's body lay partially in view, blocked by chairs. He wasn't moving. She couldn't see Big M from the camera's angle but she did spot his boots. He wasn't moving, either. There were no Ke'ters in the room anymore. They'd fled the scene of the crime.

That meant they were all on the move inside the ship.

She reached under the desk and blindly felt for the cap that protected the emergency control. Her hand trembled as she popped the shield off and pushed the button.

Red lights flashed above the Control One doors and a piercing alarm blared.

She reached up, turning on the ship-wide coms. It was imperative that she warn the crew. The alarm would let them know there was trouble. She opened her mouth—

And abruptly paused. The aliens wore language translators. She was well familiar with the devices, having learned everything about them in her classes...including their flaws.

The most fundamental flaw—language translators only worked with spoken words.

"L.O.C.K.," she quickly spelled out. "D.O.W.N.

"I repeat, L.O.C.K.D.O.W.N. The Ke'ters are attacking the crew. This is not a drill. Find S.H.E.L.T.E.R now! I repeat. Find S.H.E.L.T.E.R now. Total L.O.C.K.D.O.W.N in T.W.O."

She ended coms and let her fingers fly over the controls, preparing to initiate lockdown. It would trap the aliens and hopefully protect the crew if they made it to their quarters or an emergency shelter room. There were two on each level.

The coms on the desk buzzed and she reached over, answering it.

"Who in the hell is this? What do you think you're doing?"

She flinched, identifying Commander Alderson's voice. She'd know his shouting tone anywhere. "The Ke'ters have attacked everyone in the team leader debriefing room, sir. Big M, Mikey, and every security team leader in attendance has been murdered or seriously injured. They aren't moving."

"What? That's preposterous! Who is this?"

"Vivian Goss, sir. It's true. Mikey Miller was on his vid device with me when they attacked. I watched the entire thing go down. I'm going to initiate lockdown to seal off the ship."

"You'll do no such thing! I'm sending security to handle whatever the hell you're babbling on about, and you're going to face a court-martial for panicking the crew with your little stunt, Miss Goss."

"This isn't a stunt! It's all true! Laser fire does nothing to the Ke'ters, sir. It doesn't hurt them at all. That's the strongest weapon we have onboard."

"This is bullshit. They wouldn't attack. You were always the worst troublemaker as a girl. This is nothing more than a way to get back at me for telling you to stay away from our alien guests, and you've gone too far. You will *immediately* stop this nonsense and report to the brig. How dare you—"

She cut coms and repeated her earlier message, spelling out most of the words to prevent the aliens from understanding her intent.

The coms line buzzed but she ignored it. Instead, she watched the clock.

Two minutes passed—and then she initiated lockdown.

Sharp alarms continued to blast through the speakers all over the ship, and she knew emergency doors were being sealed, corridor access points were cut off by thick blast walls, and every venting shaft would go into crisis mode. They would seal off to prevent oxygen leaks in case of explosions but would pump in enough filtered air to keep everyone alive.

She turned the chair, facing the long-range communications controls. She turned them on to send a message but the device refused to give her access. She didn't have an override code, but there *was* a general distress signal option.

Vivien initiated it. The *Gorison Traveler* was in dire need of help.

The auto-distress beacon blinked as it transmitted a standard S.O.S.

She turned back, still ignoring the coms buzzing at her, and began to pull up security feeds.

Medical had been devastated. It was clear some kind of incendiary device had gone off in the huge room. Bodies lie in pieces, scattered among the charred, broken equipment.

Tears blinded her, but Vivian blinked them back. The Ke'ters must have targeted Medical to cripple the *Gorison Traveler's* efforts to help the injured. There was no longer a place to take their wounded. It also meant that poor man she'd come across in the corridor would die.

She continued flipping through various cameras on the ship to get an overview of the situation. No crew seemed to be stranded in the corridors, but she did see a few human bodies. She saw a few Ke'ters in random corridors, and also found three more trapped inside a lift.

"I hope you die in there, bastards."

She found more of the aliens when she brought up the bridge. They were eating the pilots and other crew.

That's when she remembered their intent to take over the ship. They would succeed, since they now had control of the bridge.

She reached over and flipped on the internal coms that kept buzzing at her.

"Goddamn you, Goss! You can get the death penalty for sealing off this ship!"

"The Ke'ters have the bridge." She tried to keep her voice calm, despite the panic she felt. "They are going to steal the ship, sir. They're *eating* the crew alive! I don't know what else to do. How do we stop them?"

Commander Alderson disconnected on her.

"Bastard!"

Then she thought of Donny and his wife, Maggie. He was the head of engineering. She punched in their cabin code. It buzzed until Donny answered.

"What's going on?"

"Just what I said. The Ke'ters have attacked us."

Donny muttered a curse. "Why?"

"We're food. They're eating us," she explained, still feeling sick. "Is Maggie safe with you?"

"Yes. We both made it to quarters. How bad is it?"

"The Ke'ters have the bridge, medical was blown to hell, and, um...Commander Alderson thinks I'm playing a prank."

"He's an asshat. You're not a teenager anymore, and the pranks you pulled were always harmless. No one initiates lockdown as a prank. I believe you, Vivian."

"Is there any way I can shut down the engines from a control center to stop them from flying us to god knows where?"

"Did you send out a distress signal?"

"I was able to activate the auto-distress." She glanced to her right, watching it flashing. "It's still transmitting."

"There's nothing else you can do." He paused. "Wait—you need to get to Control One."

"I'm there. Mikey sent me here. It's how I was able to put the ship in lockdown. Donny...the operator of this station wasn't here. Why would they leave their post?"

20

He hissed another curse. "I don't fucking know. They shouldn't have. Thank god Mikey is okay."

Grief knifed at her heart. "What can I do?" She needed him to think clearly. She'd tell him the truth about his best friend later.

"Control One has override ability in case of an engine fire. It would shut them all down. I'm going to have to talk you through it."

"Okay. How does it work?"

"It will vent all the oxygen in the engine compartments. They need oxygen to run, so they'll shut down immediately. But…there's a bad side to this, Vivian."

"What's that?"

"We'll be on backup power. Emergency system will kick in, so we won't die, but they'll only last four days. The engines themselves are what recharge the backup system. We're ten days from the closest space station, and I don't think anyone else is this far out. The Bassius Colony is too new to accommodate visitors for sustained periods, and I doubt they have long-range ships that would reach us."

Priorities, Big M would tell her. That's what she needed to focus on. *Deal with one mess at a time.* She closed her eyes, thinking. "Can I restart the engines if I shut them down?"

He hesitated. "Yes."

She knew what that hesitation was about. "How long do they have to be kept running before the backup system is recharged?"

He went quiet for another moment. "Twenty hours, at least. It's a huge risk though, Vivien, to give them engines again."

"I know. First priority is keeping people alive and stopping the Ke'ters from taking us farther from help. Tell me how to vent the oxygen from the engines. If emergency life support goes down before help arrives, I'll restart them."

"Fuck." He was breathing harder. "First, go into the submenu for maintenance."

Vivian took a deep breath and put her hands on the controls, briefly looking for it. "I'm in."

Chapter Two

Vivian jerked awake and stared at the screens in front of her. The Ke'ters on the bridge had done a lot of damage to the equipment while she'd rested. They were clearly too stupid to know they couldn't get the engines online via that location.

"Not happening." She groaned as she moved, her body aching from sleeping upright.

She glanced at the clock. It had been thirteen hours since she'd initiated lockdown. Commander Alderson refused to answer her calls. There was no security feed she could pull up in his quarters. All crew had privacy inside their homes.

Another alarming fact she'd discovered was that the other three control stations on the ship weren't answering her calls. They were supposed to be manned around the clock. Like Control One, they seemed to have been abandoned.

She'd also spent hours searching the ship via the cameras, and had located nineteen of the twenty-two Ke'ters. It was the missing three she was worried about.

Aside from those on the bridge, most of the others had been trapped in corridors, include six in the corridor outside the debriefing room where they'd attacked her adopted brother and father. And of course, three remained sealed inside the lift where she'd spotted them yesterday.

The number of murdered crew members had staggered her. She'd stopped counting after thirty. It was too heartbreaking. The Ke'ters had attacked various areas of the ship in teams. The ones who'd targeted medical with that bomb were probably the three trapped in the lift near that section.

She stood, stretching her stiff body, and moved into the small break room. She had access to plenty of food and drinks, so she wouldn't starve or dehydrate. There were even the pair of bunk beds for sleeping, but she had drifted off in the chair while watching the bridge.

Vivian ate a tasteless nutrient bar and chugged an energy drink. She felt more alert by the time she'd used the bathroom, splashed some water on her face, and returned to the control desk.

She sat, watching the Ke'ters tear into more panels on the bridge, fiddling with the insides. Another attempt at contacting the commander went unanswered.

"Dick," she muttered. Then she cleared her throat, activating ship-wide coms.

"I realize you're all locked in your quarters, worried about what is going on, and no one in any of the general areas is answering calls. They were mostly abandoned before the lockdown." She paused. "My name is Vivian Goss. I'm Big M's adopted daughter. I'm also the one who initiated the lockdown. Alien language devices don't have the ability to translate spelled words, which is why I was spelling out commands. To confuse the Ke'ters." She took another deep breath. "Engines are now offline, because the Ke'ters have taken control of the bridge. I won't go into detail, but those bastards aren't flying us anywhere. I hope you find comfort in knowing that. We're sitting in space waiting for help. The emergency beacon is on. Just hang in there."

She leaned forward, closed her eyes, and tried to think of what else she should say to her crew. "Many of you have met me, if you're longtime crew members. If you're new, I've been on this ship for years, since Big M adopted me. He is…" Pain choked her, and she had to clear her throat. "He *was* the head of security. The Ke'ters murdered him. I wish he were the one addressing you right now. I'm in Control One, and I promise I'm doing the best I can to keep everyone safe and alive until help arrives." She paused. "Please don't try to bypass the safety locks on your quarters, or to leave wherever you're currently located. There are some Ke'ters trapped in corridors throughout the ship and laser fire doesn't work on them. You're safer where you are."

She ended transmission and sighed, closing her eyes. The weight of every life onboard the *Gorison Traveler* was on her shoulders. The pressure felt intense and like too much to handle. But she didn't have a choice.

The internal coms line buzzed and she lunged, turning it on. "Vivian Goss here."

There was a pause. "This is Abby Thomas," a female voice said.

Vivian wracked her brain trying to identify that name but came up blank. It was a big ship, she didn't know everyone on it, and she'd been gone for two years, living on Earth while in school. "You don't happen to know the override codes for long-distance coms, do you, Abby?"

The woman paused again. "You're the operator for Control One but you don't have access? Explain that to me."

Vivian sighed. "I'm not the operator. I'm just the one in here. Do you have the override codes? I was hoping since you obviously have access to this secured number, you're maybe one of the communications officers."

"You're telling me you're *not* an operator, but you have control of that station?"

"Yes. I desperately need to send a message to the Branston Station to let them know what happened. They'll get our distress signal and send help but they'll be carrying laser rifles, which are ineffective against Ke'ters. They need to be warned."

"I have no way to verify anything that's happened. For all I know, you could be a rebel who's taken control of the *Gorison Traveler*."

Vivian frowned. "What's your job?"

"I'm not assigned to this ship. I was actually hitching a ride from the Branston Space Station to Bassius Colony to fix some glitches they've been experiencing. My parents designed most of the operating systems used on fleet vessels. I perform upgrades on them. I can get you in...but why should I?"

"Big M was the head of security."

"I've met him."

"Then I'm sure you know he adopted me. Big M bragged about his kids constantly. My father was his best friend, and he died during the battle on the *Yelton* when they were attacked by the Prog. I'm not an operator, but my adopted father insisted that his son, Mikey, and I have access to all four control stations. I was on a live vid with Mikey when the Ke'ters attacked the heads of all the security teams at a debriefing meeting. Mikey ordered me to come to Control One. When no one

26

responded at the door, I entered the access code and came in. The operator wasn't here."

"That's not protocol."

"No shit!" Vivian barked, getting frustrated. "The other three control stations aren't responding. I think they were abandoned, too. It doesn't make sense—unless they were working with the Ke'ters."

"That can't be," Abby protested.

Vivian sighed. "All four control stations were left unmanned. That's *never* done." She paused. "The Ke'ters split up and attacked sections of the ship at the same time. The team leaders of our security forces were murdered, while medical was bombed. It's gone, Abby. Totally blown to shit, and the medical personnel with it. Please don't ask me how many people were in there. I could only guess, judging by the pieces of them I've seen on the security cameras. It also means all the operating rooms, trauma bays, and surgery machines are gone."

Tears filled her eyes. "They also attacked the bridge crew and murdered everyone up there. How the fuck do you think *that* happened, huh? Let me tell you, in case you don't know—the bridge is self-contained. They have blast doors and walls, and it's sealed at all times. The only way the Ke'ters gained access was if *someone let them inside*."

"Fuck," Abby muttered.

Vivian pulled herself together. If the woman truly worked on operating systems, she'd understand how bad the situation was.

"The good news? If any of our people *were* working with them, the Ke'ters probably ate them. I've located nineteen of the Ke'ters, and every human they could get their hands on were ripped open. No humans are running free in the corridors. Nearly everyone followed lockdown procedures and got to their quarters. But three Ke'ters are missing. I'm hoping—as grim and horrible as this sounds—that maybe someone walked out of their quarters before I sent the warning and were attacked, possibly dragged back inside, and that's where the missing ones are. Trapped with their dead victims. Private quarters don't have security cameras. I can't check each one. It's really anyone's guess where the missing Ke'ters are, though."

"Why would Big M give you access to a control center?"

"Are you familiar with what happened to the *Hail Nine* transport?"

Abby cursed softly. "Yes. A rebel group set off a bomb on the bridge and took out the entire crew of six, including the autopilot computer. Over ninety passengers were left with failing life support and no way to access the backup systems since they didn't have authorization codes. They couldn't even send a distress beacon. If the transport hadn't been late arriving to their destination, if the Rainer Colony hadn't sent ships out to check on it, those people would have died for certain."

"There have been uprisings on some of the colonies. I'm sure you're aware of that, too. You said you were on your way to the Bassius Colony. It's brand-new and still closed to visitors while they make certain it's fully operational. That's also partially to prevent any rebels from attacking while it's still vulnerable and staff is limited.

"Big M gave me override codes to all four control centers in case something ever happened to the security on this ship. He wanted to make certain our people wouldn't end up like the passengers on the *Hail Nine*. But besides knowing how to turn on the auto-distress beacon and disable the automated cannons to avoid blasting any rescue ships, I can't do much more than view what's happening in common areas. I'd like access to long-range communications to send a message to the Branston Space Station to let them know how dire our situation is, and what they'll face when they can get help to us. I watched the Ke'ters attack on a live feed. Our laser rifles only messed up their uniforms. They didn't even damage their scales."

Abby remained silent for long seconds. "You said the engines were offline. Why?"

Vivian fought to retain her patience. Though frustrated, she understood the woman's distrust. "The Ke'ters have control of the bridge. They were going to fly us to their home world to become food. That's what I heard one of them say when I had an open vid link to the attack on the security team leaders. I contacted the head of engineering, who's a friend, and he talked me through opening the exterior vents to pull the oxygen from the engines. It shut them down. It's a temporary stall. In three and a half days, backup systems will go down, including life support. I'll have to allow the engines to come back online to keep everyone alive. And that means—"

"The Ke'ters can fly us wherever they want," Abby finished.

"Yes."

"Fuck!"

Vivian bit her lip. "You want the truth? Help isn't going to be able to reach us in time. At best, if you give me access to long-range communications, I can send a message to the space station to let them know what's happened and who's responsible. The Ke'ters thought they

29

could fly the *Gorison Traveler* to wherever they wanted. I fucked up their plan, but that could mean their ships are coming *here* now. If they are, they'd be able to target our transmitters and easily take them out."

"Yes, but you have the ship on lockdown. It's going to make it damn hard for a boarding party to reach everyone in their quarters."

"I'm aware. It will buy us more time, but I still need to tell someone about the Ke'ters, especially the part about laser rifles having no impact. That's what every security force carries. Otherwise, the rescue teams are just going to become more food to these bastards."

Abby remained silent.

Vivian was starting to get desperate. "I need your help, Abby Thomas. I'm not a rebel. I'm a cultural specialist."

"Alien-race expert?"

"Yes. I just graduated. This is my first post. Lucky me."

"I guess you didn't see this attack coming?"

"I wasn't allowed near the Ke'ters or asked for any input from Commander Alderson. Have you met him?"

"Unfortunately."

"Then you know how he is. He didn't give me this job. Big M raved me up to one of the admirals he knows, probably asked a favor to get me assigned to the *Gorison Traveler* to keep our family together. I just recently got assigned here. The commander was pissed. He had some old buddy handpicked for this job, but when I asked Professor Regal about him, she'd never heard of him before."

"Professor Regal?"

"She's basically in charge of all information collected on alien races. She sends cultural specialists updates to keep us current. This guy wasn't even on her radar, which means—"

"He doesn't actually know much about aliens," Abby cut in. "Got it. Met the type. Set in his ways and doesn't care to learn anything new." She paused. "It's a thirty-two digit bypass code. You better be for real, Vivian Goss. I'm risking my ass by trusting you. Keep me updated. That's all I ask."

"You got it." Vivian turned in the chair, facing external coms, and put her hand on the digital pad. "I'm ready."

She followed Abby's directions, carefully punching in each number. The long-range transmission station came fully online, giving her access. "I'm in. Now what?"

A hail beeped loudly. Vivian jumped, startled.

"Answer it," Abby urged.

She did. "This is the *Gorison Traveler*."

"Earthling, this is Brassi Korack. I'm from the Veslor home world. My ship is the *Brar*. We received your automated distress signal and have tried numerous times to hail you. We're four hours from your location. What is your emergency?"

She was shocked. The Veslors were aliens from an unincorporated world. Little was known about them, but she'd read up on what information they had. The voice was male, very guttural sounding, and held a slight growl.

"Who?" Abby whispered, reminding her that they hadn't disconnected.

Vivian swallowed and muted the hail to talk to Abby. "They're a shifter race who trade with one of the space stations out in the ninth quadrant. From what I've read, they live by an honor system. You know, their word is their bond. They have a great reputation for being honest. They're four hours away. Maybe they can help us."

"The guy sounds dangerous. Are we allied with them?"

"No."

"Damn."

The Veslor began to speak again. "Hello, Earthling? Are you there?" The male paused. "Have we lost them? I thought they were receiving finally."

Someone snarled words the translator didn't pick up.

"I'm going to talk to them to feel them out," Vivian decided. "I'll call you back." She ended the call with Abby, muted the incoming ship call buzzer, and activated her mic once more to exterior coms.

"This is Brassi Korack," that guttural voice repeated. "Are you having communications issues? What is your emergency? Are your systems failing?"

She leaned forward, putting her elbows on the station in front of her. "My name is Vivian Goss. I'm on the *Gorison Traveler*. I just gained access to external communications and am still figuring them out. I apologize for the delay. I'm also surprised to be speaking to Veslors. I was told you mainly stay in the ninth quadrant."

"That's true, but we had business in this section of space and heard your distress beacon. We ran long-range scans, only to find no other vessels are nearby. I debated on hailing you. Earthlings normally snub us, but it would be heartless to not offer help if it's needed. We have compassion."

"You're traders, right? What would you ask in exchange for assistance?"

He hesitated. "Gratitude would be nice, but not necessary," he said dryly. We're seeking alliances. We'd like to expand business to other quadrants. Earthlings have expanded considerably. Doing a kind deed might open doors for us."

"I'm not a person of influence who could help you in that way. I'm sorry. All I can do is promise that I'll try my best to talk to someone about it in fleet."

"Understood. We'd still like to help you. Some of my males are good with repairs. Your position hasn't moved. Have your engines gone down? We have some spare parts aboard if needed. No payment necessary."

"I took the engines offline." She debated briefly before continuing. "Twenty-two Ke'ters boarded our ship, but ten days into our journey with them, they attacked and took control of the bridge. Cutting engines was the only way I could stop them from flying us to wherever they want to take the ship."

He snarled viciously. "Ke'ters?"

He spat the word as if it were vile, and his anger was clear. They had something in common, if the Veslors didn't like the lizard race. "Yes."

"They *eat* other races. Why would you trust them?" He paused. "They'll fly you to one of their outposts, enslave your people, and use them as a food source."

She flinched. "We're aware of that now. I didn't make the decision to let them onboard. I'm dealing with the fallout."

"Fallout? I don't know that word."

"Um, the consequences. Your English is pretty good."

"I downloaded your language from the distress call. It was simple to decipher."

"Wow. Your computers are amazing, then. I thought I was speaking directly to you."

"You are, Vivian Goss. We have implants. I learned your language in seconds with an instant download to my mind."

That surprised her; it was something she didn't know their race was capable of. It implied some of their technology was better than what United Earth had access to.

That part *wasn't* a surprise.

"Our laser rifles were useless against them."

"Their skin is tough."

She nodded, then realized he couldn't see her. "Do you mind if we do a visual? I'd like to see who I'm talking to."

"I don't mind."

She tapped on the panel, located the camera and waited. In seconds, he accepted the transmission, and his live image came on the monitor in front of her.

The sight of him took her breath away. She may have read about Veslors, but had never seen what they looked like.

Brassi Korack had a very manly face. It wasn't quite human, though he had similar features—two eyes, one nose, and a mouth. But he had slightly animalistic traits. His golden eyes were like nothing she'd ever seen. He had thick black eyelashes to match the long mane of hair she could see. The sides of his head were either shaved or he didn't grow hair there. His ears were pointed, his skin dark. The brightest, lightest thing about him were his eyes.

He studied her back intently. "Hello, Vivian."

It reminded her that she probably looked like crap. She had slept upright in the chair for maybe an hour or two, and hadn't even brushed her hair afterward. She glanced down, realizing she was in the comfy jumpsuit she wore in her quarters. It was pale blue in color, shapelessly covering her from her neck to wrist to ankle, and was about as unsexy as an outfit could be. "Hello, Brassi. It's nice to see you." She smiled briefly.

He leaned in closer. "Your teeth."

She ran her tongue over them, hoping something wasn't stuck. "What about them?"

"They're small, and not sharp. Apologizes. I was just surprised. You're the first Earthling female I've ever seen." His gaze roamed her face. "You appear fragile and tiny."

"Thank you?" She wasn't sure how to respond to that. Was he insulting her or just making a general assessment of her appearance? She recalled what her professors frequently cautioned about first contact with alien races. Misunderstandings were bound to happen and to never take offense. All ego should be set aside to properly learn their customs.

Veslors were normally far away in the ninth quadrant. It wasn't surprising he hadn't seen any human women out there. Human fleet ships only sent males that deep into space. A few alien races in that area were known to steal and sell females for sexual slavery. Fleet wasn't willing to risk a war if any members were taken, and it would make United Earth look weak if they didn't try to recover lost female members. They just avoided the risk altogether.

The Veslors weren't on the list of avoid-at-all-costs species known to be doing anything so heinous.

She glanced at his lips. They were wide, and appeared a bit pouty because of their fuller size. He opened his mouth—and she tried to hide her reaction.

"You definitely don't have small or smooth teeth. They look dangerous and sharp."

He chuckled and smiled, revealing more of them. "You appear frightened, Vivian. No need. Veslors never harm females." His humor vanished as quickly as it showed. "It's cowardly to hurt someone incapable of defending themselves equally." His eyes flared with emotion that looked similar to anger. "Cowards have no honor. Veslors don't tolerate such species. Do Earthlings?"

"My race has honorable *and* dishonorable people. It varies by person. But I have honor."

"You have good and bad people?"

"Yes."

He cocked his head, studying her with those golden eyes. Then he smiled again. "You're very honest. Most races wouldn't admit some of their kind are flawed."

"Humans can be very flawed." She thought of the commander. He was a total dick.

"Long ago, in the very distant past, my people were the same. We fought each other for stupid, greedy reasons." He blinked a few times. "Then other races came, and we learned to work together to save our planet and people. We recognized the flaws and deceptive ways of other races, learned to detest those traits. It made us better as a whole. We pride ourselves on honor and truth now. The dishonorable are quickly removed from our ranks."

She understood what he was saying. They'd evolved to a point that it was probably extremely shameful to be a shithead in his culture, and they didn't abide by it.

"Do you need our help, Vivian? We offer it with compassion and no deception. No race should be eaten by the Ke'ters. They are cruel, unfeeling creatures."

He looked sincere—and she made the decision to trust him. "I'll be honest with you again, Brassi. I'm just a female whose job is to learn about and profile alien races for the people who make decisions." She raised her hand, motioning to the room around her. "It's not my job to run stations or send out distress signals. I ended up here when the Ke'ters turned on my crew. I'm not a fighter, though I was trained to defend myself against attack. But I don't know how to save my people from the Ke'ters."

She leaned in close to the screen. "Either I turn the engines back on, and risk the Ke'ters transporting us to their home world. Or we're all eventually going to die while waiting for help from our own people. They're too far away to reach us before our backup system goes down. I want to trust you so badly because I'm desperate. My crew is depending on me to save them, and to make the right decisions. I can't offer you anything of value. Knowing that, will you help kill the Ke'ters? And also promise not to hurt humans or take over this ship if I let you onboard?"

He appeared shocked, since his eyes widened. He blinked a few times before masking all emotion from his face. "We don't steal ships or enslave other races, Vivian." He grimaced slightly. "And we are rather exceptional at killing Ke'ters. They've attacked some of the planets in our system in the past, attempting to capture our people. We slaughtered the invaders."

He lifted his hand, and she watched as sharp, long claws grew from the tips of each of his four fingers and thumb.

"We're able to rip through their hard skins. Their greatest weaknesses are their necks, and we also have weapons that will blow holes in them. I give you my promise—we'll board your ship, exterminate your Ke'ter problem, and then leave. No harm will come to your people. I don't want you to die at their hands. It's an agonizing way to go."

Tears filled her eyes. "Thank you. Please hurry."

He turned his head, growling at someone. Then he faced the screen again. "We're coming, Vivian. Are you safe where you are? I can give you fighting tips if need be."

"I'm locked in a secure room. They can't get to me."

"Good. I ordered my pilot to fly to you as quickly as possible."

"Thank you, Brassi. I'm going to take our auto-defenses offline to allow you to dock with us, and I can manually override each section to allow your crew access to where the Ke'ters are trapped." She paused, trying to recall first-contact procedures for face-to-face meetings. There was nothing normal about what was about to happen. "We breathe oxygen. Is that going to be a problem for you?"

"We've been on your Earth stations and had no difficulties. We'll be wearing armor to protect us against the Ke'ters. They include life support in case of chemical attacks. We'll be fine."

She felt relief for the first time since the attacks began.

"I'm having all my men download your language to help them communicate with your survivors. Please ask them not to attack us."

"Of course. Again...thank you, Brassi."

"I'll contact you when as we make final approach to ask where you'd like us to dock."

"Okay."

He stared at her with those golden eyes, gave her a nod, and a slight smile. "We'll be there soon, Vivian. Be safe."

He ended coms, and she sagged in her chair.

What if she'd made a mistake by trusting the Veslor?

Did she really have any other option?

The answer came quickly. *No.*

She turned on the sound for incoming calls. It immediately buzzed. She figured Abby wanted an update and answered.

"You fucking bitch," a familiar voice slurred. "I'm going to see you court-martialed!" Commander Alderson laughed. "You ruined everything—and for what? Because I wouldn't let you talk to the fucking Ke'ters? Big Mike isn't going to be able to protect you anymore, little girl. You've fucked yourself almost as badly as this assignment. You stole my ship and ruined our chances with the Ke'ters!"

"They *attacked* us, sir. People are dead. The Ke'ters are eating people, Commander. I'm not joking. This isn't me being a sullen, silly teenager. I'm an adult. I wouldn't lie about something this grave."

"You and your fucking pranks!"

She took a deep breath. "I admit, as a teen, I did some things I'm not proud of. But it's one thing to set up motion sensors in the corridors to make farting sounds as people pass by, or put pink dye in the laundry washers. I would *never* lie about dead people or aliens attacking us."

"Bullshit! You were always trouble. Wouldn't be the first time you made me drink. Pink fucking outfits on our security officers... You don't forget something like that."

She ground her teeth together, frustrated. "You're drunk, sir."

"You bet your ass I am. That's because I'm locked in my quarters and can't get out!"

"Sober up. Hopefully, you'll be back in charge soon if things work out." She hung up on him and reversed the call from Abby to reach her quarters. It was time to update her, and then she'd have to make another ship-wide announcement.

They would soon be boarded by the Veslors.

Chapter Three

Vivian turned on ship-wide coms and tried to remember the speech she'd prepared. The Veslors should be arriving at any time.

"This is Vivian Goss again. I have good news. A rescue party is on the way."

She didn't want to say too much, or warn the Ke'ters about who they were about to face, even though they were trapped. It wasn't as if they could flee or take hostages, since they'd already eaten any humans they had access to. But Abby had agreed with her about discretion when they'd talked over what to broadcast.

The Ke'ters were likely thinking it would be a long time before that rescue team arrived.

"Once the Ke'ters have been rounded up, we'll go section by section to check on everyone and slowly remove lockdown. Just hang in there, and if you hear weapons fire at some point, don't be alarmed. It's the rescue team."

She blinked back tears, choking up with emotion. "Many people have died. I want to prepare you for that once lockdown is over. There are bodies in some of the corridors. Medical has been destroyed, so avoid that area. It's not safe. There's massive blast damage. Every crew member assigned to this ship has specific training. Some of you are going to need to use your skills to help reestablish order. Just remain calm, don't panic, and if any remaining medical personnel could meet in Cafeteria Two, it

41

should be large enough to run a triage area. If you're injured, go there once your section is cleared. Thank you."

She ended the broadcast and sighed, hoping the crew and passengers would listen. Most of them were going to be shocked when their rescue team ended up being unknown aliens instead of other humans, or even an allied alien race. She'd handle that situation later.

The external coms beeped and she spun in her chair, accepting it. "This this Vivian. Are you ready to dock?"

"We're approaching from the front."

She glanced toward a panel. "Auto-defenses are down. Come in on the port side of the ship, to cargo seven. I've made it easy for you to find. I've also depressurized it. When you dock, wait for me to ensure it's safe before you unseal your doors. Otherwise there won't be any air waiting for you."

Brassi chuckled. "That was smart. We see the hole."

It probably looked like that to him. She watched the camera closely and saw a dark ship approach the open cargo doors.

Commander Alderson would have a fit if he knew she'd not only allowed unallied aliens to dock with them, but she'd basically opened doors into space inside a cargo hold. Donny had suggested it to her when she'd called him, swearing those large cargo holds were designed to take an exterior breach if they were sealed off from the rest of the ship first.

The Veslor ship docked with the *Gorison Traveler*, completely encompassing the open doors. She tapped on the controls, sending air back to that section once it read the breach had been sealed. It took a full minute before it was pressurized again.

"It's safe," she called out to Brassi. "You've got air and sensors are reading that your ship has secured the breach. I'm opening the interior doors, and the blast ones I had to seal leading to me. Just follow the corridor."

"We're on our way, Vivian. I'm eager to meet you in person."

She was scared shitless. There was only one way to discover if the Veslors were truly trustworthy. That meant putting her own ass on the line first.

Vivian had overridden the door lock to Abby's quarters and let the redhead out. Then, using security cameras to check each corridor, she'd opened blast doors and monitored Abby's progress as she made her way to Control Three. They'd gotten her to that station and safely inside, where she now could watch the camera feeds and take over if Brassi had played them.

Vivian ended the call. "You heard him, Abby."

"I'm going to throw up. What if they lied?" The other woman sounded nervous.

"Then you're the one in charge instead of me. I'll be dead. Just remember what I told you about the engines. I've transferred control for the vents to your station. You can bring the engines online and take them back off once the backup power has recharged, if this goes wrong. You also know how to reach Donny now."

Vivian worked as she spoke, opening the blast doors along the corridors between her and where Brassi's people had docked. There was a Ke'ter they needed to deal with in one corridor, but she'd already warned them about it during a previous com.

"What do I do if these Veslors *do* kill you? Then we'll have two hostile alien groups on the ship."

"You seal the blast doors again to trap them, in that event. We spoke about this. What choice do we have? You and I are strangers, too, but I'm trusting you. It's called having some faith in desperate times."

"Right. I'm not going to let you down, Vivian. I see them. They're on the ship moving your way... What in the hell?"

Vivian glanced up at the monitors. "I see them, too. Brassi said they had protective armor. I'm guessing he's the one in the lead."

There were six large forms, wearing black uniforms that covered them from the tops of their helmet-shielded heads to their large boot-covered feet. They carried rifles, each sporting multiple wicked, deadly-looking blades along the tops of the barrels.

"Damn, they look big and scary, don't they?"

"You said they can shift forms? Into what? They could pass for really large humans. Look at the body mass on those guys."

"They have the same basic shape as we do but their features are slightly different, if you could see their faces. The information wasn't clear about what they can shift into. I'm guessing this is their primary form." Vivian was suddenly glad she'd been able to take a quick shower and put on a spare uniform while Abby had learned how to work Control Three. "Fair warning, I'm going to look ridiculous when you see me, once I leave Control One. Whoever had stored spare uniforms in the locker is far larger than me. I'm clean, though. I thought it would be bad to do my first face to face with the Veslors if I stank from body odor. I've sweat buckets with all the stress I've been under."

Abby gave a nervous snort. "I'm not sure if that was a good idea or not. They look dangerous, and you're a woman. They might want to fuck you if you're as young and attractive as you sound."

"I'd rather they want to do *that* than kill me at this point." She tensed as they approached a Ke'ter. "Shit. Are you seeing this?"

"Those Ke'ters look *so* creepy," Abby whispered.

Vivian tensed as the lead Veslor dodged to avoid a blast from the Ke'ter's weapon. It hit the wall, leaving a burn mark, but it didn't penetrate the hull.

The Veslors charged the lizard alien, not even shooting their weapons. Instead, they twirled them, using the blades to effortlessly deflect blasts.

The one she thought might be Brassi leapt forward, almost hit the ceiling of the corridor, and came down right in front of the Ke'ter. The Veslor struck fast, the blades of his rifle hitting the Ke'ter in the throat.

The head came off and the body dropped.

"Gross!"

Vivian silently nodded, agreeing with Abby. "The body's twitching."

Another Veslor came forward and shot with his rifle, hitting the downed alien center mass to the chest. A hole appeared in the Ke'ter's body, and the alien stopped moving.

The group of Veslors walked around the two pieces of the dead alien, advancing her way.

"They can certainly fight. Okay. It's time for me to go out there."

"Are you sure about this, Vivian? We could send them to handle the threat first."

"We need to know if we can trust them before giving them access to our people. I'm putting in my earpiece now. Do you have yours?"

"Yes."

Vivian shoved the small metal device into her ear and pressed it on, cutting coms to Control Three through her station. "Can you hear me?"

"Loud and clear," Abby said in her ear.

"Here I go. Wish me luck."

"You're crazy brave. Good luck."

Vivian stood and strode to the doors, opened them, and stepped into the corridor. She heard heavy booted feet approaching as the doors sealed behind her. Her heart pounded as she stepped into the center of the corridor, facing the direction the Veslors were coming from, but she spared a glance up at the camera. Abby would be watching her.

She forced a smile and did a slight thumbs-up before her body tensed again. She fixed her total focus on the curve of the corridor. At any second, the Veslors would round it.

"You look good," Abby whispered in her ear. "But that uniform dwarfs you. It looks like you had to roll the legs and arms. How tall *are* you?"

"Are you trying to distract me?" she whispered.

"Hell yes. My knees are knocking from fear, and I'm the safe one right now. You're completely vulnerable."

She smiled for real, amused. Time was up though when a huge, black-shelled body came into view. He stopped abruptly, and the large bodies following almost slammed into him. He lowered his weapon, careful not to point it at her. She tried to calm her breathing down from an outright pant due to fear.

"Brassi?"

He reached up, touched the helmet, and the plating over his face opened. Relief hit when she recognized his features and those golden eyes. He approached until he was mere feet from her. "Vivian." He lowered his gaze down her body. "You *are* small."

He had to be close to seven feet tall, and really wide. His chest alone looked like a mini tank, with that armor. She started to hold out her hand but then halted. "Thank you for coming. I hope none of you were injured dealing with the Ke'ter?"

"We're fine," a gruff male voice growled from one of the others.

She glanced at them. They completely blocked the corridor, their faces covered, but she got the impression they were all taking her measure. She focused on Brassi again. "I thought I could lead you to where the Ke'ters are located." She slowly lifted her hand, pointing out the camera. "We'll be tracked by those, and the blast doors will be opened as we reach each section we need to go to."

Brassi stepped closer, and she had to tip her chin up to look into his eyes. "I don't want you leading, Vivian. You look extremely fragile. Our suits are impregnable against Ke'ter weaponry. Your body is not. You will stay behind me and use me as a shield. When we confront the enemy, allow one of my males to protect you until the danger passes. Don't fear

47

them if you're grabbed and pinned to a wall. It will make you a smaller target, almost impossible to hit if we cover you."

She nodded. "Okay. I'm not going to argue. You're better prepared for this than I am. I've already admitted I'm not a fighter. I have a little training but I'm out of my depth with lizard aliens. The one I fought was bad enough, and I caught him by surprise."

He reached out fast, and she gasped as his large gloved hands wrapped around her upper arms. "You fought one? Are you harmed? We have a medic with us."

His men shifted around and a black-clad figure stepped forward from the group. He held a weapon also, but carried a pack in his other hand. "I'm Vassi. Where are you injured, female?"

It was surprisingly touching that they cared and were prepared to treat her. "I'm not hurt."

Brassi let her go and stepped back, his gaze traveling down her body once more. "You fought a Ke'ter but weren't harmed?" Brassi sounded shocked, and his golden eyes widened.

"I kind of snuck up from behind and jumped on his back while he was, um…eating someone. I used a tactical knife and shoved it into the back of his head, at the base of his skull. Then I stole his weapon and used it on him when he began to move again. I shot two big holes into his body. I've checked on him. He hasn't gotten up. I'm pretty sure he's dead. We're going to have to pass him and his victim on our way to the lift to reach other levels."

"You are deceptively harmless in looks," Brassi mused, but he grinned, showing off those sharp teeth of his. "Interesting. I'm impressed with you, Vivian."

"I also mentioned I'm desperate. Humans often find the strength to do things they normally couldn't in order to survive."

He cocked his head. "I appreciate that you're still being truthful with me. I hope it continues."

"I won't lie to you. You have my word." She held his gaze. "We need you and your team, or the people on this ship might not survive until our own come. Some of the people we'll free are going to do or say stupid things out of fear when they see that a human team hasn't come to our rescue. I wanted to warn you."

He grinned again. "This shall be fun, then."

She waited but he didn't say more. "Okay. Let's deal with the three Ke'ters stuck in a lift." She glanced up at the camera. "Bring the lift to this level but don't open the doors until my say so." She turned, heading toward the nearest closed blast door in the opposite direction that the Veslors had come. "There are a few bodies beyond this door."

Brassi grabbed her by the shoulder, his touch firm but gentle. "Stay behind me, Vivian."

She'd forgotten. "Of course." He wanted to shield her. He put himself in front of her, with his men grouped closely together at her back. A chill ran down her spine but she ignored it. Trust had been given, and she didn't have time to second guess her decisions now. She needed to have faith the Veslors wouldn't hurt her.

49

"Here we go," Abby whispered in her ear. "The lift is coming to Deck Seven. The Ke'ters inside have their weapons aimed at the doors. Be careful."

Vivian had almost forgotten their com link was open and Abby could not only see her, but hear everything. "Thanks." She relayed the information to the Veslors.

Brassi stopped as he rounded the corridor. She peeked around him, seeing the bodies on the floor. It was where she'd attacked the Ke'ter. Brassi motioned for her to stay back as he proceeded forward, crouching near the alien lizard body.

"It's dead."

She joined him. With Brassi crouched, she was taller than him but not by much. Veslors were seriously huge. The smell in the corridor wasn't as bad as she'd imagined it would be, considering the two corpses left rotting for about eighteen hours in the previously sealed section.

Suddenly, the human medic's body twitched, and she gasped, her gaze locking on him. The man's chest rose and fell. Nausea swamped her. "He's still alive!"

She was grabbed by slightly rough gloved hands on her upper arms and moved aside as Vassi, their medic, moved past her. He stepped over the Ke'ter's body to crouch on the other side of the human on the floor. She watched closely as he opened his pack, pulled out a scanner, and ran it over the human.

He snarled a word that didn't translate.

Brassi responded in that growly language.

50

Vassi spoke again and put the scanner away.

Brassi turned his head to peer at her. "Your human still lives but there's nothing that can be done for him. His lower vital organs have been eaten, and the Ke'ter who fed from him filled his body with changing spit."

She frowned. "Changing spit? I don't understand."

Brassi hesitated. "A substance from their mouths that invades the flesh and bloodstream. It will keep the victims alive for long periods but they can't be saved at that point."

Vassi shoved the scanner inside his bag and stood. "This human is no longer quite as human as before. The spit changes the organic composition of the body to keep it preserved. Is that the right word? Ke'ters only eat live food. The spit makes their victims live longer, but the missing organs can't be replaced. All the tissues are infected and won't heal. There's no coming back from this. Was that clear?"

"Oh fuck," Abby whispered in her ear. "So basically, they're saying the Ke'ters secrete something that changes DNA and there's no cure."

"I got that," Vivian whispered back. She stared at Vassi's covered face, wishing she could see his eyes. "Is he suffering?"

"Yes. The victims tend to wake from the pain on and off. The preservative keeps spreading, and its agony. Victims can last for days in this state before they die."

It broke Vivien's heart. She'd promised to bring the crew member help. She had...but they wouldn't be able to save him.

Brassi got her attention when he yanked the tactical knife out of the dead Ke'ter, examining it.

"That belonged to my dad," she told him.

He wiped green blood off the blade on the Ke'ter's uniform, and then offered it to her handle first. "You took one down with this? I'm even more impressed, Vivian."

She accepted it and carefully used a snap strap on the uniform pants to secure it to her side. "Thank you." Her gaze went to the downed human. His fingers twitched and a low groan came from his lips. He didn't open his eyes though. She couldn't imagine his suffering.

She looked at Vassi. "Can you give him something to stop the pain, at least?"

He shook his helmet from side to side. "No medicines will work now. The preservative has spread through his tissues. We've tried many drugs but none helped to ease the pain."

"You know what needs to be done," Abby sniffed, sounding as if she were crying. "You heard them. You need to show mercy to that poor guy. Use your knife."

"I can't." Vivian forced her gaze off the injured man. "Don't ask me to do that."

"Vivian?" Brassi stood, staring down at her. "We've asked you to do nothing."

"Not you." She tapped her ear. "Abby thinks I should put him out of his misery. Kill him. I can't." She shook her head.

Brassi glanced at her ear, looking confused.

She pulled out the earpiece. "It's a com device. I'm linked to another woman who's helping us move around the ship. Her name is Abby." She shoved it back inside her ear.

Brassi gave her a look of compassion. "I'll end the male's suffering, if you wish. It would be a kindness."

"No." She reached out to touch his chest plate. "It could be seen as an act of war when this is all over, if you were to kill a human. We'll send help back to him once lockdown is over, and the ship's medics can tend to him. It shouldn't take long. He's unconscious right now. I hope he stays that way."

Brassi nodded.

"Thank you, though. For offering. I appreciate it." She shoved back her emotions. "Next step is dealing with the three Ke'ters trapped in the lift. They're armed and ready to fire." She pointed. "Just around that corner. You let me know when to tell Abby to open the doors to let them out."

"Stay back here." Brassi reached up and the plating over his face sealed, hiding his features again. "Vassi will stay with you."

She watched the rest of them move forward but they stopped at the curve.

"Let them out," Brassi ordered.

"You heard him," Vivian stated. "Open the lift doors, Abby."

Vassi stepped closer, grabbed Vivian around the waist, and in the next instant, she was pinned to a wall by the big guy, her feet dangling.

Fear flooded her, but he didn't do anything other than keep her secured in place, using his body as a shield.

Loud blasts sounded as the Veslors and Ke'ters clashed. Something screamed.

She clutched at the hard-plated body against hers and ducked her head even closer to Vassi.

Then came silence. He gently lowered her to her feet.

"The enemy is dead," he informed her. "It's over."

"All three Ke'ters are down," Abby confirmed. "The Veslors look unharmed. Their armor took a few shots but I'm not seeing any damage."

Vivian was relieved. She felt responsible for the Veslors. They were on the *Gorison Traveler* because she'd begged them to come help. It would be her fault if any of them died defending her crew.

One of the big Veslors came back around the curve of the corridor and opened his face plate. It was Brassi. He smiled.

She gave him one back. "None of your men are hurt?"

"No." He tapped his chest. "Good armor."

"I'm glad."

"What's next?"

"There are six trapped in a corridor on the second level." They were the bastards who had killed Big M, Mikey, and the rest of the security team leaders. "A few are trapped individually, and then there's the ones on the bridge. Three could be locked in private quarters, since I couldn't find them on the security cameras...but realistically, they could be on the lose."

"You mentioned them." Brassi motioned her forward. "Avoid looking at the bodies. You seem to have a soft heart, Vivian, and the carnage is gruesome. The only way to be certain a Ke'ter dies it to remove the head or a heart shot. We like to do both to be certain."

She glanced at the one she'd killed. It had a big hole in the head. That one wasn't ever getting up. "I'm not going to throw up. Better a dead Ke'ter than a live one."

Brassi chuckled. "Humans throw up when they see dead?"

"Some of us do."

"I've been warned."

Chapter Four

Brassi motioned Vivian to follow him, and she did. Vassi stayed at her back. The rest of the Veslor team were checking over the dead aliens, removing their weapons. She didn't protest when they took them. It wasn't like she could pay them for their help. Maybe they could sell the weapons later. They were traders, after all.

"Anything else on this level that we need to handle?" Brassi glanced back.

"No. We'll take the lift to Deck Two. There're a few blast doors sealed between the Ke'ters trapped there and where we'll get out."

"We aren't going to be fighting immediately?"

"No."

Brassi got into the lift, and she stepped in beside him. His men followed. With their size, she found herself pressed tight against him to make room. It was crowded as the doors sealed. The lift slowly dropped.

"I think I'm doing pretty good," Abby said in her ear. "It's one thing to install these systems but another to run a station. Not to mention, this one is at least ten years old. Talk about outdated. Remind me to tell Commander Alderson to upgrade when this is over."

"You're doing a great job."

"Thank you," Brassi replied.

She had been talking to Abby, but it certainly applied to the Veslors, too.

The lift stopped and the doors opened. The corridor stood empty as they exited. Vivian pointed to the right. "The Ke'ters are trapped behind two blast doors that way."

Brassi glanced at the now closed lift. "Can anyone use that to sneak up on us?"

"No lifts on the ship will move unless Abby allows it. She's controlling everything from a security station."

"Stay here with Vassi then, Vivian. You're not wearing armor. Allow us to handle the threat."

"Listen to him," Abby urged. "I have eyes on them. Stay where it's safe."

"Okay," Vivian told him.

Brassi closed his face plate. "Tell the female to allow us to near the Ke'ters."

"On it," Abby said. "Tell him to motion to the cameras when he's ready for me to open the last blast door. I'm opening the one nearest to you now. The six Ke'ters are lying down."

Vivian relayed the information to Brassi, wishing she'd grabbed an extra earpiece for him so he could hear and speak to Abby directly. But she hadn't thought they'd split up. She'd planned to stay with the Veslor group every step of the way.

Vassi moved her against the wall and put his big body between her and the blast doors that slid open to reveal more corridor. "Stay put."

"Will do," she agreed. "Do you guys have a way to talk when you're apart?"

"Yes. Our helmets allow us to stay in contact with each other." Vassi adjusted her until she was farther behind him and lifted his rifle, prepared to fight if any Ke'ters got past the others. "Do not move, female. Even if a firefight breaks out. My armor can take the hits."

"Thank you, Vassi. And you can call me Vivian."

"They are at the second blast doors," he said. "Brassi is motioning for them to open now."

She instantly heard sounds of fighting in the distance. She hated that she didn't know what was going on. "Abby? Talk to me."

"Shit is hitting the fan! The Ke'ters reacted *fast*. It's hand-to-hand combat. Our aliens seem to like that better, I'm guessing, since they're using the blades on their guns instead of just shooting them." She gasped. "Gross! Head off on a Ke'ter. Now another one. Our aliens are slaughtering them."

Vivian breathed easier. These were the ones who'd killed Mikey and Big M.

"It's over," Abby sighed. "Our aliens look fine but the Ke'ters are all dead."

Vassi lowered his weapon. "We can move now, Vivian. Stay behind me." He glanced back at her before walking forward.

She followed. They came to the scene of the battle and she avoided looking at the bodies, instead glancing at all the Veslors. They looked exactly the same in their armor. Only Vassi was easily identified because of the pack he carried.

One of the big men came toward her. She relaxed when Brassi's helmet opened once more. She liked seeing his face.

"None of us were harmed. What's next?"

Vivian was torn. There were more Ke'ters to take care of...but she had to know for sure. "I need to make a stop first." She turned from the group and heard them following her all the way to the doors of the debriefing room.

"Open it for me, Abby."

"Why? There are bodies inside."

"Please?" Vivian hugged her waist. No Ke'ters were in there. She'd viewed the room plenty of times on the security monitors.

A big body pressed to her back. It was Brassi. "What's inside?"

"A lot of dead people." She *hoped* they were gone, at least. She hadn't seen any of them moving around. "I need to make sure, though."

"Shit." Abby softly cursed. "Your family is inside there, aren't they?"

"Open the door, Abby."

"No. I'm not going to allow you to do this to yourself. I can see into that room. Wait until this is over, and then you can view the bodies after they've been cleaned up by whoever's job it is to handle our dead."

"Open the fucking door, Abby!" Vivian ground out.

"What's inside?" Brassi gripped her shoulders and pulled her back, forcing her to look up at him.

"My brother and dad were attacked in there. I need to make sure they aren't suffering. I couldn't get a really good view of either of them from the security cameras. The angles were bad." Her voice broke. "I need

59

to make certain they aren't like that man we had to leave behind on Deck Seven."

Brassi motioned to one of his men, and they pushed her back. He found the camera and looked up at it as he aimed his weapon at the sealed doors. "Open it, please. We'll protect Vivian."

"Fuck," Abby cursed loudly in her ear. "You're going to need therapy later. Don't blame me."

"Thank you." Vivian tried to prepare herself as the doors slid open.

There was a bad smell in the room, and it had her wincing and breathing through her mouth. Brassi and his men entered first, weapons drawn. She followed, stepping into the room slowly.

There were bodies everywhere. It tore her up to see people she knew strewn on the floor, a few of them partially lying on the chairs where they'd been attacked. She moved toward the podium first, where Big M lie.

She stepped around the podium. He hadn't been eaten, but she could tell he was dead. She stared down at him, her heart breaking. At least he was at peace now. It looked as if his neck had been broken, based on the odd angle where he sprawled, and dried blood had pooled on the floor behind his head. She glanced up at the wall where he'd been thrown, seeing more blood there as well. He hadn't stood a chance.

She spun away, fighting a sob, and smacked right into a big shelled body.

Brassi put his arm around her. "Is that your brother?"

"Father," she got out.

"He's not suffering, nor was he eaten. That's a blessing." His big gloved hand rubbed her back lightly. "You shouldn't see this."

"I have to check on my brother." She moved away from him and had to pick her way around fallen bodies, avoiding looking at them too closely. Mikey was in the very back, up higher where the seating was. He'd retreated there as he'd fought.

She caught sight of him around some chairs—and froze.

She couldn't see much of him yet, and wasn't certain she could take it. The camera views had been bad enough, but reality was much worse than a screen.

Brassi moved to her side. "Is that him?"

"Yes."

"I'll check on him. Don't do this, Vivian."

"I need to make sure he's not suffering."

Brassi sighed. "I would do the same." He stepped forward, moved around a chair, and crouched. A low snarl came from him, and he lifted his head, meeting her gaze.

His golden eyes appeared sad. "Let me end this for him...for *you*."

She rushed forward, understanding what he meant.

Mikey wasn't dead.

She shoved a chair out of the way, almost tripped, and then was at her brother's side. His eyes were closed and blood stained his face. The damage to his uniform revealed he'd been ripped open from rib cage to pelvis, the same as some others. She gagged but fought it back, grabbing his still hand and inching closer, staring at his face instead.

Mikey breathed shallowly.

"Vassi, come now," Brassi snarled. "Vivian's brother is alive."

"Oh shit," Abby muttered in her ear. "He's alive still? I can see enough to know he has to be in bad shape."

"He is," Vivian admitted.

The medic rushed to their side. Brassi moved out of the way, and she held some hope as Vassi ran the scanner over her brother. She looked up at his face plate, waiting until he was done.

He lowered the scanner. "I can't help him," he growled, so low she barely heard him. "The preservative is present in abundant amounts."

Vivian felt her heart shatter and a stabbing pain pierced her chest. She leaned in close to Mikey's face. "I'm here," she whispered. "I'm so sorry." She stroked his hair with her shaking hand.

He startled her when he moaned quietly. Vivian straightened, half horrified that he might have heard her.

Then his eyes opened, and she gasped.

"Mikey!"

It took him seconds to focus on her. She knew the instant he recognized her. The hand she held tightened on hers.

"Vivian."

"I'm here, Mikey."

"Run," he croaked. "Get to Control One."

"I did. Help has come."

He turned his head, staring at Vassi, still crouched next to him. Mikey looked confused, then alarmed.

62

"They're friends. It's okay." She stroked Mikey's hair.

Her brother looked back at her. "Ship safe?"

"Yes. You saved us. I got to Control One just like you told me to, initiated lockdown, and was able to cut off the Ke'ters and trap them," she informed him. "The ones who attacked you are dead. They paid, Mikey."

He groaned, agony twisting his features. "Hurts bad."

Tears spilled down her cheeks. "I know. I'm so sorry!"

He stared into her eyes, and more pain twisted his features. He moaned again, and his hand tightened slightly but still felt weak. "Tired."

"I know. You rest. You saved the ship, Mikey. I love you." She fought back a sob. "You're the best brother ever."

Tears filled his eyes. "I'm dying. It's okay, Vivian. You don't need to lie."

She normally would have laughed but instead a sob broke from her. "You're the best. I'm right here with you. I love you."

"Love you too, brat." His eyes closed, and he moaned in pain once more.

Vassi softly growled, and someone crouched at her back, pressing close.

"Let me help," Brassi rasped softly in her ear. "He could last like this for hours or days, suffering. We can't fix him. Your people can't fix him. I'll make it painless."

Tears kept falling down her face as she looked at Vassi. "You're certain we can't do anything?"

"Certain. Apologies," the male whispered. "I understand how difficult this is for you. Brassi is my brother. I would end his suffering if he were in this condition."

Brassi. Vassi. She should have guessed they might have a close relationship, with such similar names. She stared down at Mikey. He seemed to have passed out again but his pain was obvious from the way his mouth tightened, lips pressing together. He groaned again, louder this time. His hand trembled in hers.

"Not you, Brassi," his brother said. "Let me. The female needs no reminder that you were the one to end his suffering."

"Wait." Vivian fought down another sob. "Turn off the cameras to this room, Abby."

There was a pause. "Got it. Hang on." Seconds ticked by. "They're down. No feed is being recorded in the room. I'm so sorry, Vivian. It's the right thing to do. I'd want someone to end my suffering. I'm sure your brother does, too."

Vivian leaned down and pressed a kiss to Mikey's forehead. "I love you. Tell Dad I love him, too. You'll be together again." She turned into Brassi, still keeping hold of Mikey's hand, and buried her face against his shelled chest. "Please do it, Vassi."

She couldn't watch.

Whatever he did, it was indeed fast. Mikey's hand went utterly limp in hers and stopped trembling.

Brassi wrapped his arm around her waist and stood, breaking her physical connection with her brother. His other hand cupped the back of her head to make certain she couldn't look at Mikey again. He carried her as if she weighed nothing, walking them through the room. She gripped his shoulders, keeping her eyes closed, until he lowered her to her feet in the corridor.

"We're out of there. It's done. He didn't suffer."

She released him and wiped at her nose, sniffing. "Thank you."

Vassi joined them in the corridor. "Apologies, Vivian."

She forced her head to turn to stare at his helmet. Then she lifted her hand and covered her mouth. "No. Thank you. Never apologize for what you just did for me, since I couldn't do it myself. But if you're ever questioned, say I was the one who ended his life. The cameras have no sound but they can read lips if the feeds are reviewed." She lowered her hand.

"That's why you're covering your mouth," Brassi guessed.

She gave him a nod. "I'll grieve later. Are you ready to kill more Ke'ters?"

"Give us a moment," Brassi ordered his team.

After his men walked away, moving out of sight around the corridor, Vivien was surprised when the big male lowered to his knees in front of her. He reached up with both hands, completely removing his helmet, then set it and his weapon on the floor.

She stared at his pointed ears and his black hair. Brassi then removed his gloves.

"What are you doing?" She was more curious than alarmed.

He surprised her further by touching something near his throat, and there was a slight clicking sound. The armor over his chest and down each arm parted slightly. He slid his fingers into the crevice and opened it farther, removing the upper portion of his armor to reveal his muscled chest and arms. His dark skin appeared almost luxurious, with that thin, soft-looking fur covering it. She wouldn't have even noticed it if they weren't so close to each other. He had humanlike nipples, dark gray ones, and lots of abs.

He placed his armor on the floor, and then rose to stand in front of her.

Her mouth was open slightly, and she closed it abruptly. He might be different from humans, but not all that much. It sure wasn't enough to stop her from admiring his body. Any other time, she might have been more appreciative. At that moment, grieving for her family, she was more stunned than anything.

"Do you want me to turn off the cameras?"

She ignored Abby. "Brassi?"

"I'm baring my skin to you. It's what we do to show respect, when someone bares themselves to *us*. I just witnessed your intense pain. I would reveal all of myself, but for the cameras." He glanced at one, before looking back at her. "I offer you comfort."

"I think he means sex," Abby breathed in her ear. "That's *so* fucking hot! Worst timing ever for a guy to hit on you, I get that, but I'd let him comfort *me*."

Vivian reached up and tapped off the coms, silencing the other woman's commentary. "Thank you."

He opened his arms to her. "We hold each other while we grieve. Cry, Vivian. Let out the pain. It helps. I'm here for you."

She stepped closer, hesitated for a long moment before wrapping her arms around his waist and closing her eyes. He was so tall. It put her basically at his nipples, her cheek between the flat disks on his chest. His skin had a soft texture, like velvet, yet it was firm, and also super warm. It felt so nice, so comforting.

He hugged her back, holding her close, and rested his chin on the top of her head. She heard him take a long inhalation, and was glad for that shower she'd taken.

They just stood there, and she breathed him in as well. He smelled really good, like no scent she'd ever encountered before. Maybe, if she had to guess, like a warm, sunny day, with a slight hint of berries. It was soothing.

"Do you have a male?"

His soft words broke the silence after a few minutes. She shook her head.

He squeezed her a little tighter. "Good."

She eased her hold around his waist, hating to let him go, but they couldn't stay there forever. Even if she wished otherwise. He let her go, and she peered up at him. Those golden eyes of his were narrowed a little, and the way he looked at her in that moment made him even more appealing. It was as if he thought she was special.

"Good?"

He made a low growling sound. "Yes. Good. No male has claimed you as his mate."

Those sounds of his were pretty sexy. "You take mates?"

"*A* mate. One." He glanced down her body. "For life."

It was getting hot in that corridor, and it had nothing to do with the temperature. "You don't have a mate?"

"No. Do humans not take a mate?"

She shook her head. "We sometimes marry. It means making a legal contract to be together, usually have children, and live together."

He grimaced and bent, putting his armor back on as she watched. "It sounds cold and emotionless." He sealed the armor down his arms and along his chest, hiding his body from her again. It was a shame, since he had such a great one. He paused, holding her gaze. "Mates are much better. There's passion and intense feelings."

"I believe you." She did. Brassi had a lot of both, and he hadn't hid them from her since they'd met. The Veslors weren't an emotionally detached race.

He smiled. "We'll talk of this more later." His gaze traveled down her body again. "I'm very eager to learn everything about you, Vivian."

She reached up and clicked on her earpiece again. "I look forward to that, too."

"To what? You have *got* to tell me later what was said!"

Vivian ignored Abby as she watched Brassi put on his gloves and his helmet. He closed the shield over his face. He lifted his weapon last, and then motioned her toward where his men had gone.

Vivian walked in front of him. She was learning the Veslors liked to keep someone at her back. It might be an alien thing they did to everyone, or perhaps it was just females. A protective thing.

The males all stood leaning against the walls just around the bend. She blushed, wondering if they'd been able to hear what was said. It wasn't as if she could see their expressions to take a guess.

Vassi straightened first from his relaxed stance and nodded at them. "We're ready when you are. What's next?"

"The bridge," Vivian answered. "I just don't know how to get the Ke'ters to come out. It's pretty secure. We can't override the doors there."

"It's a design flaw, in my opinion," Abby muttered. "I told my parents that there should be an override code added for the bridge doors when we created the security systems, but my father and the decision-makers said no."

"Just take it off lockdown from our side and maybe they'll open up if we make some racket at the doors," Vivian suggested. "We'll figure it out when we get there."

Brassi touched her shoulder.

She stared at his helmet. "I was talking to Abby. The bridge doors are locked from both sides. We can release the locks on the exterior side, but they need to open them from the inside to come out. Otherwise, they could remain sealed inside until they run out of food and water. That could take weeks."

He remained silent for several long moments. Then asked, "Can you remove the air in there?"

Vivian wasn't sure. "Abby? Do you know?"

"No such luck," the woman responded.

Vivian shook her head. "We can't do that."

"Get us there, and we'll think up something." Brassi sounded certain.

"Let's return to the lift. We're going all the way up to Deck Ten. That's where the bridge is located."

Chapter Five

Vivian stopped their group before they reached the bridge doors. "Once we round that bend up there, the Ke'ters will be able to see us on the monitor near the doors."

"You're certain?" Brassi remained close to her.

"I've been up there dozens of times, so yes, I'm sure." Vivian thought about it. "They can see the corridor on a large screen. It's a security measure when changing shifts. The doors won't open until someone inside views and confirms any visitor. No surprises that way."

"How did the Ke'ters gain entry, then?"

She looked at Vassi to answer him. "I wish I knew. I'm guessing maybe the commander ordered someone to give them a tour of the bridge, and they attacked once inside. That's pretty much the only time anyone who doesn't work there officially gains access."

"Unless they bribed someone with a shit ton of money to betray us and let them in," Abby added.

Vivian didn't want to mention that option to the Veslors. It didn't matter anyway, since every crew member currently on the bridge had been eaten. Whoever let them in had already paid for their crime, if that was the case. "My dad mentioned once that there's an option to backtrack footage to review what happened anywhere a camera is recording, but I didn't have access to do that. All I could see was the live feed. The control centers have access to two cameras inside the bridge in case of a catastrophic event."

"Catastrophic event?" Brassi questioned.

"You know, if a bomb went off or the bridge stopped responding for whatever reason." She paused. "There's no sound, of course. The cameras are positioned in places that don't pose a security risk in the case of hackers. But there are views inside to check on the condition of the crew if shit goes wrong."

"Only an admiral can open those doors." Abby paused. "DNA verification. We're screwed if the Ke'ters don't open up, since I checked the crew and passenger manifest. We've got no admirals onboard. Commander Alderson won't even have access, or I'd suggest getting him. Do you want me to release the lockdown from your side?"

Vivian glanced around at the armor-wearing Veslors. "Abby wants to know if she should unseal the doors on this side. It means they can come out if they want."

The men growled at each other, discussing options. At least she assumed that's what they were doing. She hated that they weren't talking in English, and wondered why. It was in her nature at times to be suspicious, but she'd been given no reason not to trust them so far.

Brassi viciously snarled, stepping closer and putting his hand on her shoulder. He seemed angry at one of his men, in particular.

"What are you saying?" She stared up at him.

He stopped snarling, took a deep breath, and blew it out. "Kavs suggested we use you as bait. I told him no."

Vivian thought about it. "It's not such a bad idea, actually."

Brassi released her shoulder and opened his face plate. She shivered at the way he glared at her. "No. You will not be put at risk, female."

Vivian held up a finger. "Abby?"

"You're not seriously considering it, are you?"

"I have a plan."

"No," Brassi insisted.

"Fuck no!" Abby hissed in her ear.

"Hear me out. The Ke'ters attacked us...what? Eighteen, nineteen hours ago? They killed and fed off the bridge crew. I figure they would probably love to grab me." She waved her hand down her body. "Fresh meat."

"Are you *insane*?"

"What are you *thinking*, female?"

Vivian flinched from being yelled at by both Abby and Brassi at the same time.

"Abby can distract them by closing the engine vents. They'll see the engines coming back online. She could then open them again right away, so they can't move the ship, but while they're busy, I'll run up to the door, push the button to let them know someone wants access to the bridge, and then run out of sight. They'll see me, since there's a good seventy feet of corridor in their view. I'm betting they'll come after me. Again...fresh meat." She kept her gaze locked on Brassi. "You and your men will be waiting for them right here."

"No!" Brassi snarled, still looking pissed. "They move quickly, faster than you do."

"You want to play ding-dong ditch with the Ke'ters? I'm with the big hot alien on this. It's nuts," Abby muttered. "It also won't gain us access to the bridge if all of them come after you. We'll still be locked out."

"You're right, but it also means they can't fly us anywhere. We can bring engines back online, and with it, full power to life support. We'll have plenty of time for our people to arrive. Including an admiral who can get in there with his precious DNA match."

Abby sighed. "Fuck. If it works, it would be great for us...but you could die. What if a Ke'ter gets ahold of you?"

"What is the other female saying?" Brassi asked.

"You can see inside the bridge, Abby. Is a Ke'ter anywhere close to the door?"

Abby paused. "No. Maybe ten feet from it."

"What are you talking about with the other female?" Brassi demanded, gripping her shoulders.

"Abby can see inside the bridge. They don't have someone near the door. She can warn me if that changes."

"We'll storm the doors and challenge them," Brassi said. "Ke'ters hate us as much as we hate them. I told you they have attacked our colonies. We've slaughtered all who've tried. Their pride will demand they fight us. We'll take off our armor to look less threatening."

It was Vivian's turn to get mad. "No! I brought you here, asked for your help, and I'm not risking you or your men that way. Your armor stays on. I've seen what their weapons can do. I shot one of the assholes with his own gun. It made fist-sized holes." She shook her head. "Nope. We'll go with my plan."

"Shit," Abby muttered.

"*No.*" Brassi glowered at her with those golden eyes of his.

She appreciated that he didn't want anything to happen to her. It certainly proved he cared. "It's a good, solid plan. You seem to know more about Ke'ters than I do. They killed the bridge crew right away. Will they want fresh meat if they think they can grab me? Be honest."

Brassi's eyes narrowed, but he finally gave her a sharp nod. "Yes. One could feed off a body for days, but the fresher the kill, the better tasting...or so we've estimated from their past behavior."

"Abby, go into the maintenance controls I gave you access to. Get ready to close those vents to flood the engine compartments with oxygen. Once they come online, reopen the vents to shut them back down, but not until you tell me how the Ke'ters react."

"Shit! I'm officially stating for the record that I hate this plan. But I'm doing it. It's going to take a few minutes. I'll let you know when the vents close."

"Keep me apprised of any Ke'ters going near that exit door, too."

"You don't even have to mention that part. It's insanity, Vivian. I hope to hell those short legs of yours can run faster than mine. It's why I never joined our military or fleet. I couldn't pass the physicals."

"I don't like this plan."

Vivian kept her gaze locked with Brassi. "I'm doing it. Prepare your men. When Abby says it's time, I'll run to the bridge doors, push the button to let them know I'm there, and then haul ass back to you and your team."

"Haul ass?"

"Run as fast as I can. Don't worry. I'm motivated to be faster than the Ke'ters."

He growled, turning to his men, issuing snarls their way. They began to unholster their rifles, taking positions along the walls, making a path between them for her to run through. She made a mental note to try to avoid slamming into their big bodies when she rounded the corner on her way back.

"You keep running," Brassi ordered. "Beyond us, to that point." He turned, gesturing to the other curve in the corridor. "Vassi will shield you in case any get past us."

"Got it." She felt relieved he wasn't arguing with her anymore.

"Why are there so many turns?"

She glanced back at Vassi. "In the corridors?"

"Yes."

"I have no clue."

"They're designed to give the crew a feeling of the ship being smaller than it really is, and cozier," Abby said in her ear. "Imagine a straight corridor a few playing fields long, and how intimidating that would be. They weave the corridors to prevent people from realizing just how far they need to walk around to reach various sections."

"Good to know," Vivian muttered.

"What?" Brassi asked.

76

She smiled. "Just Abby keeping me updated. She's almost ready to close those vents. The bridge will get notification through the computer when the engines begin to come back online, which the Ke'ters should be able to see or hear."

"They will," Abby confirmed.

Vivian started to stretch her body, preparing to run. The Veslors all seemed to be watching, judging by the way their helmets turned her way. She ignored them. They probably thought humans were pretty strange, if Veslors didn't have to warm up before a jog. It was okay if they found her confusing. She just wanted to make sure she didn't get a muscle cramp. That would be seriously bad while sprinting for her life.

"Alright." Abby cleared her throat. "You ready? I just have to hit one more key and the vents will close. The enemy should get notice of that within seconds, once I do."

"Tell me everything that's happening inside the bridge. Every detail." Vivian motioned to the Veslors. "Game time."

Brassi snarled. "If anything goes wrong, lie flat. We'll fight our way to you."

Play dead. She nodded. "Do it, Abby."

"Closing the vents now." Abby paused. "They're responding and closing." She paused again. "There's action on the bridge. The Ke'ters must be getting some kind of alarm. They're all rushing toward the front panel. I don't know what system that is, but I'm guessing it's something to do with the engines. The one by the door, too. He's a good thirty feet from it now."

Vivian lunged, running as fast as she could down the corridor once she rounded the curve. Two huge double doors were down there, but her focus was on the access panel.

She reached it and pressed the button, panting.

"They're turning!" Abby yelled in her ear. "RUN!"

Vivian needed no further urging. She spun and ran for her life. She heard the doors hiss open a second later but didn't look back. The corridor hadn't looked that long until that very second. She heard noises behind her and guessed the Ke'ters were hot on her ass.

A blast hit the wall, and she almost stumbled, but the Ke'ters missed her.

"Halt!" a computerized voice yelled.

She ignored it, made the curve, and kept to the center of the corridor, successfully avoiding the bulky armored bodies of the Veslors when she ran past. Weapons fire opened behind her again but she kept going, making it to the next curve.

Vassi grabbed her, and she was slammed into a wall, pinned there by his big, hard-shelled bulk. Vivian panted, her heart pounding. Shouts sounded, along with booms.

"Fuck!" Abby yelled in her ear.

"What?"

Abby didn't respond.

Vivian tried to catch her breath, listening to the fight. More weapons fire sounded, along with high-pitched screams she now identified with the Ke'ters.

Abby yelled in her ear, "All the Ke'ters left the bridge, but one of them must have realized the doors auto-close, because he spun and tried to get back in. He was too slow. He's partially trapped in the door, but alive. He's struggling, trying to wiggle back inside. They're fighting hand to hand, but nobody sees him since they're in the corridor between where you are and the bridge."

"No safeties?" That stunned Vivian. Most doors on the ship refused to close if a body blocked them. It was an auto-safety feature to avoid injuries.

"Not with the bridge doors. They close, period. Shit! That bastard is going to wiggle in, Vivian."

"Vassi!" She pushed against him. "There's a Ke'ter trapped in the doors to the bridge. Shoot him before he gets back in there!"

The big male paused, then he snarled. "Don't move." He rushed around the corner, where the fighting was taking place.

Vivian grabbed the handle of her father's tactical knife, ripped it free of the strap, and backed up. If anyone not wearing armor came around that corner, she'd have to fight. She took a defensive stance, using both hands to grip the handle. No way did she want to become Ke'ter food. A shudder ran down her spine.

"God," Abby breathed. "The guy who left you is shoving his way through the fighting and..." She paused. "He made it. He's running toward the trapped Ke'ter. Shooting now... Yes! He hit the bastard but he's still moving. He's still going to get in!"

"No." Vivian knew they'd never get the alien to come out again, now that it was clear they'd laid a trap. They'd still have to worry about whether or not he knew how to fly the *Gorison Traveler* when they brought the engines back online, after the backup power depleted.

"He shot him again... Fuck! The Ke'ter's inside. Wait..."

"Wait for what?"

"It's hurt. It staggered, now it's on its knees. It took two hits. One to the back and one to the side of the throat."

Vivian hoped it was enough to kill the Ke'ter.

Time seemed to stretch into forever in those seconds while she waited for another update from Abby.

A big body suddenly lurched around the curve in the corridor.

It wasn't covered in black armor.

Vivian gasped, momentarily frozen at the sight of the Ke'ter that rushed toward her.

Then she reacted. Those bastards had killed her father and brother.

Instead of running away, she lunged forward.

The alien stood too tall for her to easily attack his throat. Instead, she aimed lower. Basic anatomy on many aliens was the same. She dropped to her knees to make a smaller target when it swiped a hand at her with those sharp claws, and she drove the knife blade upward, nailing it in the groin.

The alien screamed.

Something suddenly hit it hard from above, and she rolled to the side, slamming into the floor and wall. The Ke'ter was down—with an armored body on top of it. One of the Veslors had tackled it from behind.

The Veslor didn't have his rifle anymore, and instead, she saw him use his hands to go for the neck of the Ke'ter.

Green blood flew, splattering her. She jerk her head away and threw up her hands, attempting to shield her eyes.

A loud snarl sounded as the scream cut off, and she finally lowered her hands, turning her head.

The armored body stood but the Ke'ter remained on the floor, unmoving.

"Are you hurt?"

She stared up at the armored Veslor and nodded. "I'm great, Brassi. Thanks for the save."

"I'm going to beat Vassi for leaving you!" He stepped closer and offered her a hand. She noticed there were tears in the tips of his glove, and it was covered in lots of green blood. It didn't matter much, since she'd already been sprayed with it. She gripped his hand and let him haul her easily to her feet.

"I asked him to. Please don't be mad."

"The Ke'ter has collapsed on his side," Abby updated her. "I think it's still alive but it's really hurt. I can see green goo spreading on the floor around it."

Brassi hauled her behind him, putting himself between her and the next corridor. Then he strode forward. She hesitated but followed.

The sight when she rounded the corner and peeked around him left her stunned.

Ke'ters were down, the Veslors were standing, but the damage to the corridor was telling. Burn marks scarred the walls and floors, along with lots of green blood. Some of the Ke'ters were in pieces. Parts of the ceiling hung down, due to blast damage. She noticed the gloves of some of the other Veslors were torn at the fingertips, as well, as if something had ripped through them. He and his men must have used their claws during the fight, to kill the Ke'ters.

"It's not moving," Abby said. "I zoomed in as close as I could. It's breathing, though."

"Shit."

Brassi turned to her and opened his face plate. "What's wrong?"

"One of the Ke'ters got back inside. Vassi shot it twice, it's down, but it's not dead. Do they have good healing abilities?"

"I don't know." Brassi's gaze locked with hers. "We kill them when we fight."

"I'll keep a close eye on the bastard," Abby promised.

"Close the vents while it's down and bring engines online. Any time they're running has to be a good thing to repower the batteries, right?" Vivian hoped so, anyway.

"I don't know. Engineering isn't my thing. I'll call your friend Donny to ask him. I'll be back. I'm muting my side but I can hear whatever you say."

"Thanks, Abby."

Brassi touched her shoulder. "How many more Ke'ters to go?"

The missing three and the single ones trapped in corridors throughout the ship had almost escaped her mind during that fight. "Not many. Are any of your men hurt?"

"We're all fine."

She felt grateful for that. "Do they need to rest?"

He snorted. "We were bored until we picked up your distress signal." He lowered his voice, and something hot flashed in his golden gaze. "Veslors have excellent stamina."

Was he hitting on her? She felt heat rush to her cheeks when she decided he was. She gave him a small smile. "Good to know."

His expression grew somber. "Are you certain you're not hurt?"

"I'm good. Promise. A little out of breath but getting back to normal. I don't run much."

"You were fast, female. Impressive with such a small body."

It was tempting to point out that any human woman would be small compared to him. Veslors were bigger than the average human...by a lot.

He left her to talk to his men, reverting once more to growls. She wished she could understand what was being said. As far as she knew, their language hadn't been added to the database yet for standard translators. Then again, she wasn't wearing an earpiece that had that ability.

"Engines are back online. Donny agreed with you. Anytime they're running is better than nothing. The Ke'ter appears to be unconscious and seriously hurt, judging by the spreading pool of grossness that passes for their blood. It kind of reminds me of sludge from solar engines when they're old. It's this goopy green color." Abby sounded calmer.

"I don't know what that looks like. I've lived on ships most of my life. I haven't ever seen a solar land vehicle up close," Vivian admitted. "I lived in a dorm at college and stayed on the grounds. But I'll take your word for it. I'm going to need another shower. Okay, you watch the bridge but we need to go after the next Ke'ter. Plot us a course through the blast doors."

"On it."

Chapter Six

Brassi allowed Yoniv to take the lead as they traversed the vessel, swiftly dispatching the few remaining Ke'ters. He wanted to keep a close eye on the little Earthling he covered from behind as Vivian followed his crew. She appeared tired but she refused to rest.

His gaze kept darting to her rounded ass, and he had to fight the urge to reach out to touch it.

The females from Earth were smaller and much less aggressive than what he was used to. A Veslor female would let him know without hesitation if she was interested in him. They tended to boldly approach males they wanted to copulate with. Not so with Vivian. It left him confused and feeling off balance. She'd allowed him to hold her, though, when he'd offered her comfort during her grief. That might be the Earthling way of showing interest in a male, if they allowed one to hold them. He really wished he knew more about her race.

"Your eyes will begin to hurt if you stare at the female any harder," Vassi called out from the front, using their language.

"Shut up," he ordered.

Kavs chuckled. "I see the attraction, too. But you'd have to be careful pinning one down. They look easy to hurt by accident."

"I refuse to discuss this with any of you." Now wasn't the time. His males could tease him later, once they were back on the *Brar*.

"I don't think these females wrestle with males to copulate."

He pondered Ruggler's words. He was their negotiator, and usually the one he took advice from when they made new trades with unknown races. He had a gift for quickly evaluating them and figuring out how they thought. "I agree. They seem too timid."

"The males of their race aren't," Nessel grumbled. "I've fought a few."

"You fight everyone," Vassi reminded him. "You like to be insulting until they attack to shut you up."

Vivian glanced back at him. "What are you guys saying?"

Her language was soft and musical to his ears. He switched to it. "We're discussing the upcoming Ke'ter we'll take on." Brassi experienced a little guilt for telling the lie but he wasn't about to share that his crew was teasing him about his attraction to her. It might make her fearful of him. That was the last thing he wanted.

"I really appreciate this." She smiled at him before facing forward again. "I don't know how I'll ever repay you for what you've done."

His gaze dropped to her ass.

Vassi chuckled, once more speaking Veslor. "There you go. Ask her for a few hours in your bed in exchange for our help."

"Shut up," Brassi snapped again. "Our king would like better trade access with United Earth. The leaders of her planet may allow us on more of their space stations for saving so many lives on this vessel. I refuse to bargain for access to her body. That's wrong."

"I bet it would feel right with her under you." Kavs paused. "If you fit. She's so small. It would be frustrating if you got her bare, only to discover that wouldn't work."

A few of his males laughed. Brassi clenched his teeth, silently promising to take them into the training room and make them regret their teasing later. He'd kick their asses once they returned to the *Brar*.

"Speak her language," he ordered. "We make her nervous when she can't understand us."

"She should be more worried about you pinning her to your bed to see if she can take you inside her. How do they even become aroused if wrestling is not foreplay?"

He snarled a warning at Kavs. "Enough!"

"Gentle touches and maybe some low growls," Vassi suggested.

His males shut up finally, probably thinking about Vassi's words and wondering how different it would be to copulate with a human female. Brassi knew *he* was imagining stripping Vivian out of her clothing and discovering how to make her feel the same attraction he suffered from.

They reached a section where the corridor remained blocked with sealed doors, and he stared down at Vivian. She stopped walking and turned to face him. Her eyes were a light green, so pretty. He found everything about her attractive, including the messy dark blonde hair that framed her delicate face and fell to her thin shoulders.

"There's a Ke'ter trapped just on the other side. Abby says he's pacing, as if he knows we're coming or something. I don't know how unless he's in contact with the survivors and they warned him. Then again, the bridge crew did rush out after me. They didn't seem to know the others had been killed, or I doubt they would have come out."

Brassi appreciated that the female shared her thoughts with him. "It doesn't matter if the Ke'ter knows we're here or not. It will die." He closed his face shield and motioned to his brother. "Protect her. Go with him, Vivian. Stay behind his armor."

"I know the drill." She moved closer to Vassi.

He felt a little jealous, wishing he could shield her small frame when a fight arose. They were his males, though, and while he'd let Yoniv head the group while navigating the ship, Brassi felt the need to lead them into battle, since he'd volunteered them to save the Earthlings. He was still angry that his younger brother had left her when they'd lured the enemy from the vessel's bridge. He understood the reason, but a Ke'ter had still managed to flee—and almost kill Vivian.

He'd felt pure rage when he had tackled the Ke'ter, unsure if she'd been harmed. All he'd known for certain was that she'd landed on her knees and the Ke'ter had tried to hit her. It had died too quickly for his tastes, but he'd just wanted to ensure her safety. He and Vassi would have had a bloody fight if she'd been harmed.

He walked to the blast doors, yanked his rifle off his shoulder where he had slung the strap, and growled low. "Open the door."

He heard Vivian softly telling the other female to do it. The blast doors slid open to reveal more corridor, and the Ke'ter quickly attacked.

Brassi lunged at it, using his blade. He hated shooting an enemy. It was too easy to take life that way. Bad blood lingered from the numerous Ke'ter attacks on their food-growing colonies, too. The elderly and the young tended to the growing fields. Not males or females trained for fighting. Attacking them was a cowardly act on behalf of the Ke'ters. He felt immense satisfaction every time he killed a member of the murderous race.

The male fired his weapon but it didn't pierce Brassi's armor. He snarled in rage and used the blade to go for the Ke'ter's thin throat. It tried to flinch away but he beheaded it fast, allowing Kavs to shoot it in the heart. It was already dead but that didn't matter. All of them had lost family to the Ke'ters at some point in the last two decades.

It was proving too easy to kill the Ke'ters trapped on the huge vessel. He returned to Vivian. "What's next?"

She appeared worried. "That was the last one we know of. The remaining three are probably trapped in crew quarters."

"What's the plan to locate them?"

She hesitated, staring up at the camera, and Brassi wondered about the female called Abby behind the cameras, opening doors and moving them around the ship. Vivian finally met his gaze.

"Abby thinks we should go to the quarters of priority crew to let them out and allow them to help us."

"Who is priority crew?"

"Abby's pulled up the night-shift security personnel and located their quarters according to rank. The day shift was on during the attack, and we lost most of the team leaders." She paused, grimacing. "Also, we should let Commander Alderson out."

He had learned a lot about Vivian in a short period of time, including picking up the ability to read some of her emotions on her face. The one she showed now seemed to be distaste. "You don't like the male. Why?"

"He's the, um, captain of the ship." She lowered her voice. "He's a total dick. When the attack happened, he refused to believe I was telling the truth. He accused me of lying."

Anger burned through him. "You're honorable and truthful, Vivian."

"Remember that talk we had about how some humans are good and some aren't? Well, I don't think much of him. He's not going to take it well when he realizes the rescue party that I allowed to board isn't one of ours."

"He'll be angry with you for letting us help?" The male sounded stupid to him.

"Big time. He's unreasonable, set in his ways—and did I mention he's a dick?" Then she looked wary. "I should warn you of something."

"What?"

"He might have me arrested. If he does, please don't interfere."

Brassi was stunned, but it quickly turned to rage. "What?"

"I wasn't authorized to enter Control One, to put the ship on lockdown, or anything else that I've done to keep people alive. I'm a civilian worker. It means anything to do with security isn't my job. I overstepped a lot of bounds and broke a lot of rules. It'll be okay, though. Once all the facts come out, I'm sure I'll be cleared of whatever charges he files against me."

Brassi didn't know what to say—but he would *not* allow her to be arrested. That meant being locked in a cell or worse. He'd seen plenty of prisoners on the colonies they traded with. The ones found guilty of crimes were frequently used as forced laborers to pay restitution.

"Really, it's fine, Brassi. There will be an investigation that might take a few weeks, but once they replay all the footage and piece together what happened, I can't see anyone wanting to put me in prison or execute me for what I did."

Now her words horrified him. "Execute? As in *kill*? You saved your people! You brought us onboard to handle the Ke'ter threat."

"I'm sure they'll realize that." She gave him a forced smile that didn't reach her eyes. "Abby agrees with me. I might be arrested but once the investigation is over, I'll be cleared of charges and released." She shrugged. "I'll just be looking for a new job. No way will Commander Alderson allow me to return to his ship."

"That's wrong." Vassi spoken before he could. Brassi agreed with his brother.

Vivian glanced between them. "We have rules. I broke them. There were extenuating circumstances, though."

"Ex-what?" That word didn't translate.

"It was a dire situation," she explained. "Rules *had* to be broken or we would have had no chance at survival. The investigators who'll have to review what happened will hopefully see that, and I probably won't be sent to trial." She paused for a long moment. "Abby says she and her family know a few admirals, and she's sure I'll be cleared, too. It's going to be fine. Just don't be alarmed if I'm handcuffed and led away, okay?"

91

He didn't know how to respond. It felt so wrong, and the idea of her being in trouble for anything she'd done angered him. "They should get down on their knees to thank you for saving them."

"*You* actually did the saving. I just broke some rules—well, a lot of them—to get you here."

"Will they arrest *us*?"

He saw her face go pale over Nessel's question. She hesitated for a long time. "Abby and I didn't think about that. It's a real concern." She paused again. "There are a few security officers I trust who worked with my father and brother for years. They're smart and reasonable. We could let them out first, make sure they're alive and no Ke'ters are hiding in their quarters, and then have you leave before we release Commander Alderson from his quarters."

"I don't like your plan," he stated adamantly. "Even three Ke'ters are a threat if your weapons don't kill them."

Vivian listened, glancing at the cameras, making it clear Abby was speaking to her. She finally met his gaze again. "Abby suggested we go door to door, speak to whoever is inside first to make sure they're human before unsealing the locks on their quarters. Anyone who doesn't answer, or who sounds like they're using a translator, will remain trapped until rescue teams reach us from the Branston Space Station. I managed to take a Ke'ter down with a tactical knife. A single Ke'ter wouldn't stand a chance against at least ten people with blades. We'll have numbers on our side, and it's not like an attack will come as a surprise now."

Brassi had to admit that sounded practical. He nodded. "I think we should stay with you until all the Ke'ters are found."

"I don't want to take the risk that Commander Alderson might order you arrested, too, Brassi. He's stupid and unreasonable when he's sober—and he was drunk the last time we spoke." She paused, glanced at the camera, and then laughed. "I don't care that I'm not hiding my lips, Abby. I meant every word I said. *He* brought the Ke'ters onboard, and he thought I was pulling a prank when people *he's* responsible for were being killed and eaten! Let him get pissed if he finds out I called him names when they review all the footage."

Brassi didn't like the idea of leaving Vivian behind if she was going to be arrested. His next words came out of his mouth without thought.

"You should come with us when we go. We can drop you off at an Earth station, after everyone realizes how you saved lives with your actions."

She appeared surprised and her eyes widened, becoming even rounder. They were definitely pretty. Then she shook her head. "I need to stay here to speak to the investigators. Thank you for the offer, though. It's going to be fine, Brassi. I'm also going to tell them how you and your men helped us. You saved all our lives." She glanced at his males. "Thank you. I can't say that enough. Not only did you save us but also the ship. That's going to mean a lot to United Earth. *Gorison Traveler* is one of their largest and most expensive noncombat personnel vessels."

She looked at the camera, listening to Abby. Then she held his gaze again. "Abby thanks you, too. Like I said, she knows a few admirals, and she promises to share how generous you've been by risking your lives. You and your people would be an asset to have as allies to United Earth.

She feels certain she can get them to agree to opening some trade with Veslors. How do they contact you?"

"Just send a transmission to our king on Veslor home world. I'll update him about what happened when we return to the *Brar*, my ship. He'll be pleased. At one time, we didn't associate with many other races, sticking to our quadrant, but times are advancing. Trade is healthy for our future." He had the urge to touch her but resisted. "Making friends is good."

She smiled. "I agree with that a hundred percent."

"Is she flirting with you? It's hard to tell with these females," Kavs whispered in their language.

"Quiet," he replied in the same tone, not wanting Vivian to be alarmed if he snarled. He changed back to English. "Good."

"I think she is," Ruggler chuckled. "You should taste her mouth to see how she responds."

He really was going to take each of them inside the training room and beat on them when they returned to the ship. He was close to his male grouping, but sometimes they irritated him. Teasing him did it faster than anything else.

Vivian glanced up at the camera. "Pull up Mitch Reese's quarters and take us there. I've never been to his place but he's one of the heads of security on the night shift. He wasn't amongst any of the dead I saw on the cameras. He's smart, was a close friend of my dad's, and he's our best bet to seek help from."

Brassi followed Vivian and his men as they entered another lift, went to a different level on the expansive ship, and then stopped outside of a door. Vivian motioned them back a few feet.

"I'm just going to signal him, have Abby unlock his quarters, and ask him to come out. Hopefully no Ke'ter is inside."

He grabbed Vivian and hauled her back, putting his body between her and the door. "That sounds too dangerous."

"He'll freak out if you're the first thing he sees." She peered up at him. "Stand at my side. How about that?"

He didn't like it but nodded.

Vivian reached up and pressed a button next to the door. "Mitch? It's Vivian."

There was no answer.

Vivian whispered, "Abby unlocked the door. We can override it to gain entry but let's give him a minute."

The door slid open—and a male in a gray uniform stood there holding a laser rifle.

He backed up, glancing between Brassi, his males, and Vivian. She slowly put her hands up. "Easy, Mitch. They're friends. I let them onboard and they've been killing Ke'ters to save us. Meet the Veslors. They're a trade race that were in the area. You can put the rifle down. I swear it's fine."

The male kept the weapon up. "What the *fuck*, Vivian?"

"We weren't going to make it if we had to wait for someone from Branston Space Station to reach us. They haven't even responded yet to our distress signal. Everything I said over the speakers when I made announcements was the truth. The Veslors aren't our enemies. Look at me," she urged.

The male glared at her.

"You've known me for years, Mitch." Sadness crept into her voice. "The Ke'ters murdered my father and brother. They smashed the back of dad's head in and *ate* Mikey." Emotion choked her voice. "These aliens came to our rescue. They won't hurt us. I've been working with them for hours while they took out the Ke'ters. The bridge is no longer under Ke'ter control. They were going to fly us somewhere to make us food. I had to shut down the engines to keep that from happening, which meant we had four days before backup power died. No life support. No power. No heat." She paused. "Engines are back online and recharging the backup. We're locked out of the bridge but that's not a problem, since no one is up there to fly us away any longer. We just need to wait for rescue teams from Branston to reach us. The Veslors *saved* us, Mitch."

The human glanced at each of Brassi's males, before staring hard at Vivian again. "You're absolutely certain about them?"

"I trust the Veslors with my life—and yours, since I brought them to you."

She quickly told the male everything that had happened, including her fear of the commander arresting Brassi and his males, and her plan to get them off the ship before allowing Alderson out of his quarters.

Mitch still seemed tense and unwilling to lower his weapon.

"What would my dad have said, Mitch? Flip the situation around and see it from their perspective. We sent out a distress signal, the Veslors responded, and I invited them onto this huge fleet vessel, saying we needed help. It could have been a trap to capture them, but they were still willing to come. They believed me, and had faith I was telling them the truth. They trusted us. Please. *Think*, Mitch."

Mitch finally nodded. "You're right." He sighed. "Alderson is going to lose his fucking mind, Vivian. I'm proud of you, though." He completely lowered the weapon to his side, seeming to no longer be wary of Brassi or his males. Then he glanced at each of them. "Thank you for coming to save our asses."

Vivian turned. "This is Brassi. He's captain of the *Brar*."

Brassi reached up and opened his face plate. "It's nice to meet you."

The male looked stunned for a split second to see his face, but then recovered. "You speak our language."

"We learned it when we heard your distress signal. Vivian shouldn't be arrested." He wanted to be clear about that.

The male grimaced. "I agree, but I'm not the commander. It will be his decision...when he can give orders again. But I can't see the brass looking at this fucking mess and letting any charges stick."

"Charges stick?" Brassi looked at Vivian for clarification.

"He thinks I'll be fine." She gave him a smile. "I'll be set free after the investigation ends. Don't worry, Brassi."

He hoped she was right. The female had done what was necessary to save Earthling lives. If her own people were too irrational to understand that, maybe it was best if Veslors didn't trade with them, after all.

He still wanted to offer again for Vivian to leave with them. That way, he could be certain she'd stay safe. He wouldn't allow any harm to come to her.

Vivian turned to the Earthling male. "Who do we get out next? I figure we should have at least five security officers with us before the Veslors leave."

"Hang on." Mitch turned away, went into another room, and returned with a few tactical blades. He kept his rifle, too, but the blades he strapped to his body. "I've got just the men and women, and their quarters are close. I assigned them to rooms close to mine for just such an event. We've been communicating this entire time, preparing for the worst. They'll be ready for a fight with the remaining three Ke'ters."

Brassi didn't like the sound of that. "You should wait for more security to arrive."

The male met his gaze. "I've been in constant contact with at least twenty of my night force since this mess started and we were locked down. We can handle the Ke'ters, now that we know laser fire won't work on them."

Vivian reached back and placed her hand on his chest plate. "We'll be fine, Brassi. Abby has our backs."

"I want more information on this Abby," Mitch grumbled. "You have an unknown civilian operating Control Three." He shot Vivian a worried look. "What were you thinking?"

"That I wanted us all to survive!" she snapped back. "I told you who Abby is. She upgrades systems for the fleet. Her clearance is probably higher than yours. I knew I could trust her the moment she had the override codes for long-distance coms, and was able to hack the internal coms to reach me in Control One in the first place. That takes skill and knowledge. It's an isolated system."

Mitch sighed. "Okay. Two quarters to the left."

They walked to where Mitch indicated. Brassi motioned for his males to stay back and allowed the two Earthlings to face the doors alone. He would trust that Mitch had spoken to whomever lived on the other side during lockdown, and that a Ke'ter wouldn't come barreling out to attack.

The male in that room was also heavily armed as the doors slid open. Mitch gave him some kind of hand signal and the human lowered his rifle, staring with wide eyes at Brassi and his males.

"These men are Veslors. They killed a bunch of Ke'ters already, and are friendlies. We're going to gather some more of our people, and then they're leaving once we're in control again. Move out, Paul. Play nice."

The male hesitated but walked into the corridor, giving them wide berth. It was fine with Brassi if they weren't immediately trusted. Vivian appeared relaxed and not afraid.

And soon he'd leave her on this ship.

It filled Brassi with regret. The short hours they'd spent together had made him want to know her a lot better.

Chapter Seven

Vivian had become increasingly nervous about the distrust the security members showed the Veslors. Mitch was keeping them in line, though. She knew she could trust him to keep his cool and not overreact—the way the commander would when he found out what she'd done. That she'd allowed a team not associated with United Earth to come to their aid.

Now, it was time for the Veslors to leave, and they'd returned to Deck Seven to see the team to their ship. Mitch had Abby release over fifteen men and women he trusted, and they grouped in front of and behind the Veslors.

Vivian was glad that Brassi and his men kept their armor in place. She'd even asked Brassi to cover his face. It wasn't that she didn't trust her own people, but she knew anyone could panic when afraid. Human nature wasn't always a good thing. She'd seen examples of that in her alien cultures classes. Some races made humans look barbaric or moronic in comparison.

They stopped outside the cargo doors, and the security members parted to make way. Mitch was the one who spoke. "Thank you for your assistance." He even held out his hand to the Veslors.

"Handshakes are a sign of respect," she informed them. She stepped closer to Vassi, the only one she could identify in their exact matching armor, since he carried his medic bag. She extended her hand and demonstrated the gesture. The rest of the Veslors watched, and then shook Mitch's hand.

Another Veslor came toward her. "It was good to meet you, Vivian." Brassi withdrew something from a holster on his armor. "This is a direct contact code to the *Brar*. Please inform me how things turn out." He paused. "Or if you wish to speak to me. I'd welcome that."

She smiled, feeling genuinely happy...but also sad. Her time with Brassi had affected her in ways she'd have to examine later, when she wasn't worried about going to prison.

She accepted the metal card with programming that included the coms code to his ship. "I promise to call. Thank you so much, all of you, for everything you've done for us." She wished she could see his face one more time, but it was safer if she didn't. Some of the security team still looked tense. "We owe you. I'll do my best to represent you to United Earth."

"For what?" Mitch asked, moving closer.

"The Veslors would like to trade with more of our space stations. I said I'd pass that information on."

Nodding, Mitch motioned to the door and it opened.

"They can't wait to get the Veslors off the ship, can they?" Abby sounded as annoyed as Vivian felt. She gave a slight nod, knowing Abby could see her on the cameras, but she didn't want to say anything aloud. Mitch had demanded she hand over her earpiece three times already. So far she'd managed to talk him into allowing her to keep it, since her and Abby were a team that had worked well together.

"Thank you," she called out to the Veslors as they entered the cargo hold, an odd depression coming over her as the doors closed.

"I'll let you know when they detach," Abby whispered. "They're boarding their ship."

"Let's free Commander Alderson now." Mitch paused. "Ask your friend if the Veslors have left yet, and then we'll move out. I'm not budging until they do."

She inhaled slowly and blew it out. "The Veslors saved us. You're acting as if we can't trust them."

"They'd be allied with us already if they were worthy of our trust. You really took a huge risk, Vivian."

"I had no choice. And it paid off. They kept their word."

"You let aliens onto our ship. It's a miracle they didn't steal the *Gorison* and cut life support to kill us all," one of the female security officers grumbled. "You were fucking lucky. You gambled with our lives. Not cool."

Vivian glared at her. "We were already good and fucked by the Ke'ters. Have you ignored the bodies we've had to pass with their stomachs ripped open, or are you just completely blind? They were *eaten*."

"This is not the time to argue." Mitch stepped between them. "Stow your shit, Yole. The outcome is all that matters now. Vivian did her best, and we're no longer locked in quarters."

"If she's telling the truth," Hugh Bark muttered. "It would be just like her to turn a molehill into a mountain and twist facts."

Vivian turned on him. They had a history. "You mean like when I wrote that report about how you harassed the shit out of me until you

102

were ordered to stay away? That was the truth—and *you* know it. You just couldn't stand that I turned you down flat when you hit on me. News flash, Hugh. You're not all that hot, and your version of pursuing a woman is actually defined as stalking."

"Stop!" Mitch ordered. "There's no longer a question of whether the Ke'ters attacked us or not. They did. We've examined the crime scenes."

Vivian sealed her lips together.

"She lies," Hugh mumbled.

"Wow, you dodged a bullet with that asshole," Abby said. "He harassed you?"

Vivian glanced at the nearest camera and nodded.

"The Veslor ship has detached from the cargo hold and is flying off. I'll admit, I was worried security would try to arrest them before they could leave."

Vivian had feared that, too. She shared most of what Abby said with Mitch. He ordered everyone to return to the lift.

They were going to Deck Four to let Commander Alderson out next. She dreaded it, but Mitch had made it clear she was to stay with him.

They reached Commander Alderson's quarters, and Mitch hesitated, meeting Vivian's gaze. "You're sure no Ke'ter is in there?"

"I told you we spoke a few times. Commander Alderson said he was locked in his quarters." Vivian also mentioned his condition. "I hope he's sobered up since then."

"Fucker," one of the female security officers said under her breath. "Glad he was having a good time while we were worried about living or dying."

"Stow that shit," Mitch snapped and pressed the button for the door.

"It's unlocked," Abby let Vivian know.

The doors parted, and a very disorderly looking Commander Alderson glowered at everyone waiting outside his quarters as he stumbled out. The door sealed at his back. He wore a uniform but it held a lot of wrinkles, and some of the buttons were undone. There were even a few food stains down the front of his shirt. If he saw any of his crew looking that way, they'd be written up and fined.

He glanced at each of them—until he spotted Vivian.

"You bitch!"

He lunged forward, stumbled, and Mitch stepped between them.

"Sir, we're in control of the ship once more. What are your orders?"

"Control? We were never in danger!" Commander Alderson blustered. "That little bitch did this to embarrass me and make the Ke'ters turn against humans." He tried to step around Mitch, his face red and his fists balled. "Do you know what you've done? The Ke'ters aren't going to share their weapons tech with us now. Hell, you'll be lucky you didn't start a war. This is your fault!"

Mitch moved again to block Commander Alderson from reaching her, staying between them. "Sir, we've toured the ship and come across crew victims, and the bodies of the Ke'ters who killed them. The threat was real."

That drew Commander Alderson's attention to Mitch. "What? Of course it wasn't! It was *her* playing a prank and screwing my career!" He stretched an arm around Mitch, trying to reach Vivian again.

She backed up and bumped into a body. One of the security members.

"Sir, respectfully," Mitch tried again, "the Ke'ters *did* attack our crew. I viewed the bodies. They were partially eaten. One of the Ke'ters still had the victim's blood on his hands and face."

He was talking about the medic, and the Ke'ter she'd killed when the attack had first happened. The medic had died by the time she'd led everyone to the Control One area on Deck Seven. That had been a very small relief, that his suffering had ended without intervention.

Commander Alderson's face paled more. "No. *No*. That can't be right. They promised to sell us weapons. The Ke'ters wouldn't do this."

"It's true," Mitch stated simply.

Commander Alderson swayed a bit on his feet. "I was going to become an admiral..."

"Is he for real?" Abby gasped. "What a shit bag. People died and he's bitching about a promotion?"

Vivian decided to ask him an important question while he was still drunk. "Sir, why were the control station operators not at their posts?"

"I don't answer to you!" Commander Alderson looked flustered. "Arrest her and take her to the brig!"

Mitch motioned with his hand, ordering everyone to hold still. "It's a valid question, sir. Why were the control station operators not at their posts?"

Alderson's expression changed to one of almost...fear? Then his face turned red before Vivian could wonder about it further.

"Follow my orders or I'll have you *all* up on charges! Take that bitch to the brig! She's still facing a court-martial. She took control of my vessel!"

"Sir," Mitch hesitated. "Answer the question."

"Fuck you!" Commander Alderson glared at him. "I don't answer to you, either. Lock her in the goddamn brig *now*."

"Are you drunk, sir? I smell alcohol on your breath."

"What?" Commander Alderson sputtered. "How dare you!"

"Under regulation six-three-nine of United Earth Fleet, I'm taking over command until you are no longer intoxicated."

"I'll see you stripped of your rank and court-martialed too! You can't do that!" Commander Alderson lost his shit and took a swing at Mitch.

Mitch avoided the punch and grabbed the commander, spun him around, and handcuffing the man.

"Your career is over!" Commander Alderson bellowed.

"He has witnesses," one of the security officers stated loudly. "You're drunk and in no condition to give orders, sir. You tried to assault the current acting head of security. I stand by his assessment. You're a mess."

More security officers mouthed their agreement, backing Mitch.

Mitch jerked his head. "Let's escort him back inside his quarters."

"You don't have permission to go in there! *No!*"

Commander Alderson looked extremely panicked all the sudden. And Vivian wasn't the only one who noticed. Mitch had one of his men grab hold of the commander then moved in front of him. "You'd rather I secure you in the brig, sir?"

"Yes! Might as well make sure your court-martial gets you at least twenty fucking years!" Commander Alderson spat.

Mitch turned his head, glancing at Vivian. "Order Abby to open his doors. She can override the locks, correct?"

"On it," Abby responded.

"I forbid you to do that!" Commander Alderson shouted. "Stay out of my quarters!"

"She's doing it," Vivian informed Mitch.

The doors slid open in front of them and Mitch stormed inside, two other security members going with him. The doors closed behind them, and Commander Alderson continued to shout and curse and make threats at everyone in the corridor, promising he'd end their careers, ensuring they'd never work on a fleet ship again.

Minutes passed.

"I wonder what he's hiding. That's how he's acting, isn't it? Or is it just me?"

"It's not just you, Abby," Vivian whispered.

The door opened and Mitch stepped out, looking enraged. He glanced around until he spotted whoever he was looking for. "Thomas, take your med kit and get your ass in there *now*. There are two injured women." He kept his body in front of the sensor on the door to keep it open. Then he shot a purely pissed-off glare at Commander Alderson.

"That's why you cleared out the control rooms, isn't it? They're the only crew able to record and make copies of footage if they wanted to blackmail you for cheating on your wife." He glanced around at his security. "The bastard smuggled on two sex workers from the Branston station. He was keeping them in a nearby room and escorting them to his quarters when he was off-duty. Then the lockdown happened," Mitch glared again at Commander Alderson, "and he clearly took out his frustrations on them. He beat the shit out of both women."

"What the hell?" Yole, one of the female security officers, stepped forward.

"It's not what it looks like!" Commander Alderson sputtered. "They're into that shit. It was just a little rough sex. I'm ordering everyone to forget this happened!"

"Fuck you, sir," Mitch hissed. "We're clearing your quarters, and then you'll be confined there."

"He should go to the brig," someone muttered behind Vivian.

Mitch shook his head. "He's a commander. He'll be confined to quarters until a higher authority takes over. You all know procedures. We're going to follow them, despite how distasteful that is. I'd love to lock his ass in a cell after what I just saw and heard from those women."

"You make me sick," Yole hissed at Commander Alderson.

Vivian was glad she was no longer the only target for the outspoken security officer when she was displeased.

Two women were led out of the commander's quarters, and Vivian was stunned by their condition. One sported a split lip and a black eye. Her clothing was torn, revealing scratch marks on her left breast and what appeared to be a bite mark. The second woman was in even worse shape. She had similar injuries, and Thomas was helping her walk, as if something was wrong with one of her legs.

Mitch unlocked the cuffs on Alderson once security had cleared his quarters, and then shoved him inside. "Seal it," he ordered.

"You're going to regret this!" Commander Alderson roared. "All of you! I'll see you destroyed!"

The doors closed to the quarters—and everyone glanced at each other in silence.

Mitch sighed, rubbing the bridge of his nose. "What a fucking mess."

"You really think he ordered the operators from the control stations to stand down?"

That was someone Vivian didn't know, probably new to the security team, maybe from the Branston station.

Mitch nodded and dropped his hand. "Yes. Or he could have fucked with their schedules to make them think someone else was covering their posts. It's the only way I can think of that he pulled it off. The operators can record copies of security footage and store it off the main computers. He probably worried he'd be blackmailed, and there would be no denying any allegations against him if they had visual proof of who was going into his quarters, and how long they stayed, when he wasn't on duty."

More curses sounded around Vivian.

Mitch glanced at her. "I have to put you in the brig, Vivian. I'm sorry. It's protocol. You're a civilian who breached secure areas, and this is going to warrant a full-scale investigation. I wish I could just confine you to your quarters, too. You'd be more comfortable there, but...rules are rules."

She had expected it. "I understand."

He hesitated. "I'm also going to have to arrest your friend."

"Tell him that's not happening. I have full clearance on all fleet ships and can prove it. Tell him to contact Admiral William Fellows, if he's in doubt. Hell, any of the top brass of United Earth, for that matter. My parents own D Corp."

After a moment of stunned silence at that revelation, Vivian repeated what Abby told him.

Mitch sighed again. "Understood. I need your earpiece now." He glanced around. "Tick, escort her to the brig, and make damn sure she's as comfortable as possible. You stay with her."

A female security officer stepped forward. "Yes, sir."

Vivian hesitated. "Thanks for everything, Abby. I'm going to pass you over now."

"I'm going to be reaching out to my contacts when the rescue teams come. You're not going down for any of this. I swear," her new friend promised.

"I appreciate that." She pulled the earpiece out and handed it to Mitch.

He accepted it and put it in his own ear. "You did a hell of a job, Vivian Goss. I'm going to put that in my report. We'll try to kick you free of any shit that comes your way."

She blinked back tears, touched by his words. "From your lips to the investigator's ears."

"This way," Tick ordered, gently gripping her upper arm.

At least she wasn't being handcuffed. The woman led her back to the lift. They had to wait for it, and Mitch asked Abby to open a route for the women to the brig, on the lowest level of the *Gorison Traveler*.

"I'm Meg Tick," the woman whispered. "I agree with Reese. Um, Mitch. You did a hell of a job."

"Thank you. I'm glad it's all out of my hands now."

Tick snorted a laugh. "No shit, right? I can't imagine having to make some of the calls you did during this clusterfuck."

The lift opened and they got inside. Vivian already missed having Abby's voice in her ear. She glanced up at the camera and gave it a sad smile, and when the lift stopped, both of them got out.

She was going to the brig. At least she knew they were kept clean, thanks to the tours she'd taken with Big M. Any cell she was put in would contain a single bunk, a thin mattress, one blanket, a sink, and a toilet.

"Commander Alderson is going down for this bullshit. He was so drunk. It's about damn time."

Vivian turned her head and studied her companion. "He's a total dick."

111

Tick snorted. "That bastard hit on me a few times, implying I could get a promotion if I blew him. As if the tiny pay increase would be worth that trauma. Speaking of tiny, every guy who acts as bad as he does owns a micro penis, in my experience."

Vivian figured Tick was trying to cheer her up. It didn't work, though, when she was locked in the cell.

"Are you hungry?"

"No."

"Me either." Tick leaned against the wall. "So you're the one who filed stalking charges against Hugh? Good for you. He hounded me, too, thinking I'd cave at some point—until I beat his ass in the training room half a dozen times. Then he decided I wasn't an easy enough target."

"He thought because I was adopted, Big M wouldn't take my word over his. He was wrong."

"Big M was a good man. Fair. I'm sorry. We all lost out with his death."

Vivian took a seat on the hard bunk mattress, and then lay down. "Thank you. I'm tired. Do you mind if I take a nap?"

"Go ahead. You've earned some sleep. I'll check over inventory down here to make sure we won't starve until we're officially off lockdown and they can get the cafeterias back open. God, I've missed cooked meals. I hate those emergency ration bars we've all been stuck eating."

Vivian closed her eyes and her thoughts instantly went to Brassi, wondering how he was doing, where he was now...and hoping she'd be able to use that card to contact him. Tick hadn't patted her down or taken it from her.

Chapter Eight

Sub-Commander Garland Shaw glared at Vivian from the other side of the bars. He was now in charge of the *Gorison Traveler*, with Commander Alderson under arrest in his quarters. He'd come to see her once lockdown had been lifted, freeing all the crew members.

Meg Tick had kept her updated. The remaining three Ke'ters had been found where Vivian had already guessed, trapped inside crew quarters. Their victims were dead and eaten. None of them had peacefully surrendered. The security team had to kill them.

Despite that, Sub-Commander Shaw's first words killed any hope Vivian had that he might release her. "You are in serious trouble."

Vivian opened her mouth, ready to defend herself.

"Excuses don't matter. You breached Control One—illegally, I might add—and initiated lockdown before our security forces could handle the situation. Then left us trapped in quarters, unable to do anything. *Then* you allowed unfriendlies aboard a fleet ship. They could have stolen it and killed everyone! You're going to be facing life in prison, if not execution."

She sealed her lips.

"That's the way I see it—as does Commander Alderson. Get comfortable behind bars, Miss Goss. This is your new life."

Without allowing her a word in defense, he spun on his heel and marched out of the cellblock.

"What a prick!" Meg whispered once he was gone. "We have over sixty dead, last I heard." She shook her head. "Reese said lockdown

114

happened less than five minutes after you'd notified security of the attack in the debriefing room. Not all of us are morons, Vivian... If the Ke'ters killed that many of us in that short of a span? Lockdown saved a lot more lives *because* you acted quickly. What made you even think to go there?"

"Mikey told me to."

"Did he give you the access codes to get into Control One?"

Vivian shook her head. "Big M did after what happened to the *Hail Nine* transport."

Meg nodded. "Smart. With the rebels acting up, it's always a real fear that they could target high-ranking crew members with access to control rooms on ships. Did Big M upload your DNA to give you bridge access, too? I heard we're still locked out. Maybe you could bargain your future with that."

She shook her head. "Only admiral DNA can do that."

"I didn't know." Meg shifted her position, leaning against the wall across from her in the cellblock hallway. "At least we finally got a transmission from Branston Space Station. They're sending rescue ships. They should arrive in about seven days."

"I hope they bring an admiral with them, or the *Gorison Traveler* will remain stationed here a lot longer since it can't be flown."

"The tech guys are trying to find a way onto the bridge. That friend of yours, Abby Thomas, is working with them."

"Good." Vivian took a seat on her bunk.

"Imagine the money her and her family are worth. I'm told ever since Sub-Commander Shaw realized who she was, he's been kissing her ass big time. She's apparently on a first-name basis with the brass. They've given her free access to pretty much any ship."

Vivian was glad to hear that. She'd hate to have Abby locked in the cell next to hers.

Meg's coms buzzed, and she answered. "Tick here."

Vivian couldn't hear what was said to the security officer, but Meg nodded. "On my way." She looked at Vivian. "They have the cafeteria up and running. I've been given permission to take a meal break. I'll return in an hour, and I'll bring you something back."

"Thank you. A hot meal sounds nice."

"No shit. I don't even care if they're just serving noodles and that white plant stuff they call chicken."

Vivian watched her go, and the doors at the end of the cellblock sealed once more, leaving her alone. She leaned back against the wall, sighing.

It had been about eight hours since she'd been locked up, and she might be looking at weeks more. If Shaw and Alderson got their way, it would be for the rest of her life. They didn't care why she'd done what she had. They seemed to be looking for someone to punish. And the Ke'ters were all dead.

The doors opened, and Vivian turned her head—standings in surprise when Abby entered. Her friend had changed outfits, and now wore some kind of loose black tech jumpsuit with a ton of large pockets, her red hair pulled back into a ponytail.

Vivian strode to the bars. "What are you doing here?"

"We don't have much time." Abby touched the coded panel and the locks disengaged. She yanked open the door. "Come with me."

Vivian hesitated. "I'm not allowed to leave."

Abby reached in, grabbed her, and yanked her out of the cell. "You're in danger! Walk and talk." She released her and spun, jogging toward the doors. "Stay on my ass and trust me."

Vivian rushed after her. "What's going on?"

"That piece-of-shit Sub-Dickhead Shaw is plotting with Bigger Dickhead Alderson to spin this entire nightmare to shove the blame on others. I hacked into their private com conversations. They're going tell brass it was *you*, as the ship's cultural specialist, who recommended the Ke'ters come onboard. And after the attack, you locked everyone in before the crew could do anything to save the ship because you supposedly panicked, realizing what a huge mistake you'd made."

Vivian was momentarily stunned speechless. "That's not true! I wasn't even consulted. Hell, I wasn't even allowed *near* the Ke'ters."

"I'm aware, of course. They're also going to blame the head of security for allowing the Ke'ters such freedom on the ship, including the tour that gave them access to both the bridge and the operators in the control centers."

Vivian felt sick. "My dad didn't—"

"I know," Abby interrupted. "They're trying to save their jobs, Vivian, and they don't care who they have to shove the blame on. Big Mike is dead. He can't defend himself. Nor can the murdered bridge crew, who were apparently ordered by the commander to give the Ke'ters a tour.

"But *you're* still here—and they can't allow you to live to testify about what really happened. They decided it would be believable if you committed suicide in the brig over the guilt of so many dead crew, because of what you and your father had supposedly done. It's why we need to get you to safety. They're going to *kill* you, Vivian."

"But...there are *recordings*! There's no way they can hope to get away with any of that bullshit."

"Sub-Piece of Shit ordered Reese to his quarters. He plans to put Shithead Commander back in charge so they can destroy any proof of what happened before and during the attack. And you'll get blamed for doing *that*, too. Assholes!"

Shocked, Vivian could only gasp.

"But I have plans for them." Abby paused, overrode the locks to gain them access to another door, and they entered the cargo area. "You need to suit up." She pointed toward the far wall and yanked a small digital pad from one of her pockets. Her finger tapped it and part of the wall opened. A spacesuit came out, hanging from a mechanical arm that stored it upright.

Vivian was still reeling from everything she'd heard. "They can't do this!"

"They can try, but they won't get away with it. I made sure of it. I changed the access codes to all four control centers. I also locked them out of the computer's core, where everything is stored—but I made backups first of the hours before, during, and after the attack, just in case. I've already sent them to a computer at home. Climb into the suit."

The suit lowered, the mechanical arm still holding it in place. Vivian frowned. "That's for exterior repairs."

"Yes, it is." Abby was tapping on her pad. "Just crouch down in the suit and when I open the exterior doors, it will create a vacuum that will propel you far from the ship."

Abby shoved the pad back into a pocket and withdrew a second device from another one. It was palm-sized, and when she activated it, a red light began blinking. When Vivian continued to stand there in shock, her friend grabbed the front of her shirt and literally began shoving her inside the uniform.

"This is a distress beacon I stole off one of the emergency pods. I couldn't get you into one, since only the bridge can launch them. The spacesuit is going to have to do to get you off the ship."

Vivian shock started to wear off...replaced by paralyzing fear.

Abby grabbed her arms and gave her a shake. "Stop standing there, damn it! I shut down all the cameras on this level but security might be doing sweeps. Get in the fucking suit, Vivian! We don't have a lot of time. Someone also might get suspicious when your guard shows up to eat while she's supposed to be on duty. I, uh...kind of relieved her for an hour, pretending to be one of her superiors."

"You want me to float in space until the rescue teams come? I don't think the suits store enough oxygen for that."

"They don't." Abby smiled.

Vivian was even more alarmed. "And that makes you happy? You think it's a kinder way to die than what Sub-Commander Shaw and

Commander Alderson might have planned for me? Why can't I just hide in one of the control rooms?"

"This will be safer for you in the long run. And...there might be a certain ship I called back, who's out there waiting to pick you up."

Vivian quickly figured out how to climb into the Y-shaped opening of the suit, which included ducking her head to get into the attached helmet before shoving her arms into the sleeves. The gloves were large, and she had to go up on her tiptoes and push her butt to the back of the suit to get her legs through the high split, which still dug into her uncomfortably until she shoved each foot into the boots. They were huge; she had shoes on, and still there was ample room left inside them.

"This doesn't fit so well."

"You don't need to walk around in it. Well, not much, anyway."

The suits were also heavy, bulky things, like body-shaped machines. She faced Abby after she got into it. "Most uncomfortable thing ever—and I'm going to have a wedgie from hell because the center leg split is designed for someone a heck of a lot taller."

"Sorry. What matters is, you'll be picked up soon."

"By the *Brar*?"

"Yes." Abby pulled out the pad. "Brace. It's about to seal, and I'm releasing the clamps. These suits are designed to be held in place during depressurization, and then release when there's no oxygen left in the room. I'm bypassing that function. Just move away from the wall once I'm gone and crouch near the exterior door."

"Wait!" She was starting to panic. "Why not just have them dock to us again to pick me up?"

"I need to blow you out, Vivian, to get you beyond the ship's auto-defense systems. Sub-Piece of Shit put them back online and is monitoring them. The defense system won't target this suit, though, since it's coded as part of the ship. This is faster than hacking our defenses anyway. He'd be aware of them going offline and would probably send security after *me*."

Vivian understood, unfortunately. "So you're actually going to blow me out of this ship?"

"Sorry. It might be a rough ride, but know that Brassi and his crew are out there to pick you up. The beacon I activated will make sure they've got something to find you with. No more time. You need to go."

"What about you? You'll be in danger if you stay."

Abby grinned. "Don't worry about me. I can handle those assholes and kept them from destroying evidence. Brace."

Vivian tensed her body and Abby tapped the pad. The suit closed from the throat under the attached helmet, down her chest and stomach, and around her legs, surprising her by tightening to fit her body shape, and then the clamp above her released. She nearly staggered under the weight of the suit but managed to stay on her feet.

She could still see Abby since the face plate of the suit was clear.

"Have fun with the sexy alien. Let him do that thing where he strips off his shirt to comfort you," Abby yelled, still grinning and backing up with her pad. "I'll contact you when it's safe for you to come home!"

121

Vivian watched as Abby left the cargo bay, then red lights began to flash in the room. She knew that was a warning that the exterior doors were about to open. Usually the room was decompressed first, the oxygen vented out. She'd done that herself when she'd prepared for the *Brar* to dock with their ship.

She turned, moving slowly to the center of the room, and turned her back to the wide exterior doors. Despite the fit, it still felt like walking in something four sizes too large and a hundred pounds too heavy for her frame. Every step she took was an effort not to trip in the bulky boots.

"Are you ready?"

The voice in the helmet surprised her. "Not yet."

"Hurry! We don't have much time. I'd like to get off this level before security finds me or realizes I sprang you from the brig. I plan to hole up in Control One until help comes, since I don't trust those bastards not to try to kill me, too, no matter *who* my parents are."

Vivian crouched, or tried to, but the weight of the suit made her fall over. She braced as she lay there. "Do it. Thank you, Abby."

"Ball up as much as possible. I'm overriding the controls to rapidly open the doors so you don't hit them on the way out. At least, that's the theory I'm working with."

"Fuck," Vivian muttered. She pulled her limbs closer to her torso and tucked her head. It was tough to do in the bulky spacesuit. "Ready."

A loud alarm blared—and then it was all motion.

She felt her body get brutally yanked in one direction, and then all light was gone briefly. The suit helmet flared with soft, dim illumination, but it was still total darkness around her. Gravity was a thing of the past, the heaviness of the suit no longer an issue. She got fleeting glimpses of the *Gorison Traveler* as her body rolled swiftly through the dark. The ship was huge at first, but as her body continued to careen weightlessly, it faded more and more as she tumbled through the blackness of space.

When she saw the *Gorison Traveler* again, it was from a greater distance.

Abby's voice came from the helmet. "Vivian? Tell me you're alive and I didn't kill you."

"I'm okay and off the ship. I didn't hit the doors. I'm not hurt."

Abby chuckled. "I knew it would work. Coms will cut out soon. It's a range thing. Good luck."

"Be careful. Are you sure you don't want to come with me?"

"I can't control the pad I'm using to hack into systems if I'm in a suit. I can only get you off the ship. I'll be fine. I'm on my way to Control One now."

"Let me know when you get there."

Silence greeted her. Her body rolled again, floating through space.

"Abby?"

She didn't answer.

Vivian got another glimpse of the ship then, even farther away. Being sucked out of the cargo hold with the oxygen had propelled her from the *Gorison Traveler* as if she'd been wearing thrusters. She'd probably gone beyond coms range.

She continued rolling, since she couldn't figure out how to stop. She stared into space, occasionally spotting the ever tinier-looking *Gorison Traveler*, until the point when she could no longer see the lights from the ship.

Only blackness and silence surrounded her for what seemed like endless minutes.

Vivian slowly began to worry when she estimated a good half hour had passed since being jettisoned from the ship.

Where was Brassi?

Fear came up as well. What if the beacon didn't work? What if he couldn't find her, or had lied to Abby about picking her up?

She calmed herself about that last part. Brassi was honest and honorable. He wouldn't say he'd pick her up if he didn't plan to do so. She needed to have faith in him once more. He'd find and rescue her.

She just hoped it would happen before the air supply in the suit ran out.

She didn't do external repairs and knew very little about the suits. They were used by specialty crew trained to work on the outside of the ship when something went wrong. She'd heard they indeed had small thruster controls, but she wasn't sure how to access them.

Vivian lifted her arms and brought them closer to the lit mask of her helmet in order to inspect them, noticing a pad on one. It was dark, not activated. She didn't dare try to turn it on. With her luck, she'd cut oxygen or open the suit by accident, which would kill her.

She tumbled very slowly now, staring at endless stretches of dark space. She couldn't really feel the motion any longer, since gravity was gone. It was weird, too quiet, and she tried to remain calm.

"Fifty percent," a robotic voice announced a short time later.

"Hello?"

The suit didn't respond.

Vivian tried to slow her breathing. Fifty percent probably meant oxygen supply. She stared out of the helmet, looking for any sign of Brassi's ship, but there was nothing.

She turned her head, continuing to search the darkness.

Minutes later, she spotted something.

She tried to focus on it but her body rolled leisurely, removing it from sight. Then it slowly came back into view. It was lights—and they were coming straight for her. It had to be Brassi and his crew.

"Brassi? Can you hear me?"

There was no response. Maybe the suit coms couldn't connect to his ship, or maybe she needed to turn them on. Not that she knew how to do that.

The lights got closer, and she made out the shape of a large ship. It wasn't anywhere close in size to a fleet ship. She just hoped it was the *Brar*, and not some vessel sent by the Ke'ters to find out why their colleagues hadn't delivered the *Gorison Traveler* and all the people onboard.

The craft had a dark-surfaced hull, few lights, and it flew right next to her, almost close enough to touch, making Vivian fear it might bump her and send her rolling in another direction. Instead, it glided past, moving slowly, until it was behind her.

A hatch opened, and she pulled her arms and legs in. Bright lights came on inside, showing what looked like a cargo hold.

"Shit." They were going to just let her float inside.

Vivian held her breath until she made it into the hold. She hit a wall, bounced, but they sealed the exterior doors before she could float back into space again.

Suddenly she began to feel a heaviness in her body, and her suit lowered to the floor. It only grew worse—until she felt as if she were being crushed by the suit against the metal floor she was sprawled upon. The lights inside the cargo hold were blindingly bright. She squinted, trying to make out anything from the limited view beyond her slightly turned helmet.

Vivian struggled to sit up, but after being gravity free, the suit felt as if it weighed a thousand pounds. Muted noises came to her...something hissing, and then loud booted feet. Someone crouched over her and hands grabbed various parts of the suit. She could barely feel them though through the thick material. She was lifted and turned over onto her back...

And then Brassi's worried face was inches away.

He snarled something and lifted his head a little. It gave her a better view, now that he wasn't in her face. Two other Veslors were crouched beside her. One of them lifted a terrifying-looking twisted blade, and she felt her body jerked a little. They were cutting off the suit.

She didn't protest, since she had no idea how to open it. She just hoped they wouldn't accidently cut *her*.

Heat seeped in everywhere they'd sliced the suit open. It made her realize just how cold she must have been in space before she was bought onto the *Brar*.

Brassi leaned close to her mask again and started to tug on the helmet.

"That won't work," she yelled, hoping he could hear her. "It's one piece. It doesn't come off. Get the suit open and I can wiggle out."

He snarled something in his language, locking gazes with her. "Are you hurt?"

"No." She gave him a small smile.

He didn't smile back. Instead he turned his head, growling more orders at his men. She felt a hand press against her stomach, there were more tugs on the suit, and then the sleeves were being torn down her arms. She curled her fingers to clear them of the built-in gloves. Hands gripped her calves and pulled her legs free. Then her body was tugged down to clear her head from the helmet.

She breathed in lungsful of the filtered oxygen of the ship. It was warm, and smelled like something close to pine trees.

Brassi dug his hands under her and picked her up, getting to his feet. She still suffered from her body feeling heavy, despite being freed from the suit, but she managed to lightly grasp his shoulder.

"Vassi is waiting in our medical bay for you."

"I'm fine."

Brassi didn't slow, snarling more orders to the men behind them as they went through a door that automatically opened at their approach. The bright lights dimmed in a hallway. It was narrow compared to the corridors on the *Gorison Traveler*. He took her to a lift, which also automatically opened. She guessed either his ship didn't have a lot of security, or it was programmed to read him and open doors at his approach.

He stared down at her face. "I apologize that you were out there so long. We were told you'd be shot out in the opposite direction. We had to keep far enough away to avoid your ship attacking us, and then circle around once we picked up your distress signal."

"It's okay. I'm just glad you came. I'm so sorry that you had to do this."

The lift stopped and the doors opened. He tore his gaze from her and walked forward.

"I can walk. I mean, I'm suffering a little gravity sickness but it's nothing compared to being in that suit."

Brassi kept walking fast down a straight hallway until he stopped and turned as another door opened.

She came face to face with another Veslor. This one had to be Vassi. He had black hair, golden eyes, and looked enough like his brother that she was sure of her guess. His voice, when he spoke, confirmed it.

"Place her on the exam table."

"I'm *fine*."

They didn't seem to care. Brassi lay her down on a comfortable bed and Vassi ran a scanner over her. He paused it above her chest and frowned. "Mechanical device."

"Oh!" She'd forgotten about that. She unfastened the top of her shirt and reached in, found it, and pulled it out. "It's the tracker Abby gave me to help you lock on to me while I was in space."

Brassi took it and turned, going to a wall. There was a slight hissing noise, and then he came back to her. Vassi finished his scan. "Her body temperature is a bit lower than it should be, elevated readings probably from stress, but overall, she's in good condition considering her recent ordeal."

"She hit the cargo wall in her suit. Yoniv tried to adjust the gravity in there to slow her down as she came in, but failed."

"I'm good," she assured them both. "Really. The suits are more like shells. They can take some damage."

"*You* can't, though." Brassi's gruff tone implied he was still angry.

She tried to sit up but her body still felt sluggish. Brassi helped her, his big hands gentle. She smiled at him again, and then studied Vassi's features. "It's good to finally see you."

He looked confused for a split second, but then grinned, revealing his sharp teeth. "That's right. Brassi was the only one who opened his face plate."

"Are you sore? You're moving very slowly."

She turned to Brassi. "It's just gravity sickness. Totally normal. I'm just glad I'm only experiencing a mild version of it."

"Gravity sickness?" Vassi turned, picked up some kind of digital pad and began to tap at it with a finger.

"Adjusting to pressurization can make some humans feel like their bodies weigh twice what they normally do. I'm not nauseous, though. I took a ship-to-ship transport shuttle once, that was overloaded. They don't turn on gravity when that happens. It was a nine-hour flight. I watched some of the other passengers puking their guts up when we docked, and some couldn't even get out of their seats. They needed to be taken out on stretchers to recover."

"Internal organ damage?" Vassi's head snapped up.

She thought about what she'd said then stifled a grin. "'Puking their guts up' is just a saying. It means they were emptying their stomach contents. Anything they'd eaten or drank came up."

Vassi nodded. "Ah."

"I just feel tired but I'll adjust fast. I'm a ship brat."

"Ship brat?"

She nodded at Brassi. "I grew up on fleet ships. The longest I've lived on a planet was in college for my cultural studies. I spent two years on Earth. I was able to take most of my courses by computer before that."

"Your parents were United Earth fleet?"

"My father was. My mom was a colonist he met and talked into marrying him. She could only take that kind of life for a year before they divorced."

"That life?"

"Living on a ship. She was used to fresh air and living on surface, and it was rough on her to be in space. She wanted to go back to the colony, to her family, after she gave birth to me."

"Explain 'divorced.'" Brassi stepped closer.

"They ended their marriage. Um, I told you we have contracts? They both agreed to end it. Dad got custody of me." She saw him frown. "When parents end a marriage, they need to decide who the child will live with. Her colony was pretty unstable still from harsh weather conditions, and they both agreed that fleet ships are better for children, with their advanced medical facilities and schools. So she left me behind with my dad.

"When I was ten, he was killed during a mission. By then, Mom had married a new man and had four more children with him. She felt I would be too much of an additional burden for them, and refused to take custody of me." That still hurt Vivian to think about. "Instead, I was adopted by my father's best friend. Big M and his son are the ones who died on the *Gorison Traveler*. They wanted me with them, and we were super close already. I grew up with them. My mom is someone I can't even remember."

Compassion softened Brassi's features. "I apologize, Vivian."

"For what? You aren't the one who refused to take me in because you didn't want an extra mouth to feed. I can't thank you enough for letting me onboard and picking me up." She dropped her gaze. "You can drop me off anywhere. I don't want to be a burden to you or your crew."

"You're welcome to stay on the *Brar* for as long as you want."

131

Vassi growled something low, and whatever he said caused Brassi to chuckle.

Vivian glanced between them. "I really need to learn your language."

"I said it's not as if you could eat much." Vassi put the pad down. "Earthlings are so tiny."

She couldn't disagree, compared to Veslors. "I still appreciate everything you've done. Abby is going to get this mess cleared up as soon as possible. I have faith in her."

"She informed me of what's going on when she hailed us." Brassi's tone turned gruff again, and fury flashed in his golden eyes. "You did warn me some of your people had no honor, and your captain is one of them. I won't allow anyone to hurt you. Consider the *Brar* your sanctuary for as long as you need it."

"Thank you."

"No need to say that. Now, you need food and rest." Brassi slid his arms under her and lifted.

"I can walk."

He ignored her once more, carrying her out of their medical bay and back into the hallway.

Chapter Nine

Brassi took her to another level and got off the lift, walking past closed doors until one at the end of another straight hallway slid open. It was decent-sized crew quarters. There were two couch-like pieces of furniture, but they didn't have backs or sides. Just long, plush-looking pads to sit on. A wall of storage took up one side, and there were two interior doors. He carried her to one of the couches and sat her down. Then he straightened and backed up a few feet.

"I have something to tell you, Vivian."

She kept her gaze locked with his, waiting.

"We don't have guest space. We must share these quarters. But you are safe with me; I promise. I'll sleep on the floor, and you can have my bed." He turned away, walking toward the far wall, and tapped a section of the storage area. It slid open to reveal some kind of machine. His body hid most of it, but soon a tempting smell hit her nose.

It was cooked meat.

She thought about what he'd said, about his ship not having guest quarters. That wasn't unheard of on smaller vessels. Some of the patrol cruisers used for the fleet were like that. Two crew members were assigned to share small, private rooms, which contained bunk beds. Each one came with a toilet and sink, and a communal shower room was used by all.

"I understand. I'll sleep on your couch, though."

He turned, holding a plate and a mug-like glass with a handle. He approached and crouched down in front of her, handing her the plate first. She accepted it. It was filled with brown meat strips and nothing else.

"Noma. I hope you eat meat. If not, I'll get you something else."

"Real meat?" That was a surprise.

"Yes. They are animals from my world. Not smart, but they are abundant and tasty. Is that offensive to you?"

"No."

"Try it."

She carefully picked up a strip of meat. It was warm, as if it had just been cooked. The machine had to be some kind of food replicator. It smelled good, almost like beef, and she took a tentative bite.

Flavor exploded on her tongue. It was delicious, soft enough to bite and chew easily. She smiled at him.

He grinned back and lifted the mug-like glass. "This is nee. Water with nutrients, and flavored with fruits."

She settled the plate on her lap, finished the meat strip she was eating, and accepted the drink. She took a tentative sniff. It smelled a bit like berries. Taking a little sip, she found it chilled, and incredibly tasty. Vivian took a bigger sip.

"I ordered Vassi to learn everything about your race, and he'll come up with more things you'll like to eat and drink. This is my favorite snack, and he's seen other Earthlings eat it before on the stations we visit. We felt this was a safe choice."

She was touched—and amused that he kept calling humans "Earthlings." It didn't matter though. He was a thoughtful man. "Thank you."

"You say that often. There is no need to show appreciation." He adjusted his body to sit on the floor, watching her. "What happened after we left?"

That killed her good mood fast. "I was arrested and put in the brig. Abby got me out of my cell, had me climb into the suit, and here I am. I deeply appreciate that you came for me, Brassi. You didn't have to. I'm sure it was a pain to turn around and come back, not to mention dangerous."

"No pain. It was a simple thing to order Yoniv to change course. We were only two hours from your ship when Abby hailed us."

She realized that meant Abby had spent hours planning her escape—and Brassi had been waiting for quite a while for her to get sprung from her cell.

"Is the noma burning you? Too hot?" He leaned in, frowning.

"No. It's perfect. I like it."

"You're doing this." He bit his lower lip to demonstrate.

"I do that when I'm thinking about something too hard."

"You're safe here, Vivian. No one will hurt you. I give you my word."

"It's not that. I *do* feel safe." It wasn't a lie. She had far bigger things to worry about than her current situation—like her future. If Abby couldn't clear things for her, she'd be wanted by United Earth as a criminal if Commander Alderson got his way. "You saved my life, Brassi."

135

He growled, anger transforming his features. "Abby said your people were going to kill you. I don't understand why. You did nothing wrong, and you hailed us to help them."

"Commander Alderson was the one who arranged for the Ke'ters to come aboard the *Gorison Traveler*. He brought them onto our ship, and they attacked us. That whole mess is *his* fault, but he needs to blame someone else. Otherwise, his career is over. Abby learned that he was going to destroy all the evidence of what really happened and make it seem like everything was my fault."

"The Ke'ters attack anyone they want to eat. And that would be any race not their own. They also never do what anyone else wants. Are your people that stupid?"

She nodded. "Some of them are. Commander Alderson must be pretty desperate right now. Not only did he let the Ke'ters onboard, but he also allowed four control centers to remain unmanned. Regulations state that they're to have operators around the clock. That alone is reason enough to be fired."

"Your people died, but he's worried about keeping his job?"

She liked how Brassi cut through it to get to the point. "Yes."

"What is the importance of the control centers?"

It wasn't exactly classified information. Anyone could look that information up if they wanted to. "Control centers have access to most of the ship's systems. A control station operator's job is to watch over everything on the ship. They usually split up levels to watch, but all control centers can access any camera regardless. They're also a safeguard in the event of something catastrophic happening. Like, say, if

136

our ship was attacked." She arched her eyebrow at him. "I took over Control One, put the ship on lockdown, and was able to shut down the engines even though I wasn't on the bridge."

"Your people fear attacks like that? Do they happen often?"

She shook her head. "No, but they could. We have some trouble with rebels from time to time. They haven't targeted large fleet vessels, though. Security is too tight on most of them. But there's a fear that maybe they'll start using small ships to fire on us, get in a lucky shot, and take out the bridge. You can't fly the *Gorison Traveler* from a control center, but you've got access to all the main systems in an emergency, to help keep the crew alive until another ship could arrive to give aid."

"Why do you have rebels? Are they from other races who hate yours?"

"No. They're actually United Earth residents." She ate another strip of meat and put her drink on the floor, since there wasn't a table. "UE has settled colonies on a lot of planets and opened tons of space stations. Some of the residents get upset over late supply shipments, or they feel they aren't given enough resources to flourish. I understand and sympathize with their plight. It shouldn't be that way. Then again, it makes no sense to me that they'll complain about a late supply shuttle, and then blow it up in retaliation when it *does* arrive. Supplies are just delayed even longer then, until a replacement shuttle can be sent. That's not helpful to anyone, including the people the rebels say they're doing it for."

"That's hurting them."

She nodded and finished her food. "Thank you."

137

He stood, taking her plate. "Stop saying that."

She bit her lip. "I was raised to be polite. At least I'm not calling you 'sir.'"

He came back to her and sat on the floor. "Sir?"

"It's a form of respect for someone in charge. You're captain of your ship. Protocol would dictate I only speak to you when you ask me a question, and to finish my answer with 'sir' at the end."

He just studied her.

"Like this, sir. Thank you, sir. No problem, sir."

"That sounds silly."

She chuckled. "It's a good thing I didn't decide to become a fleet member. I took a civilian job, but the 'sir' was still required on a fleet ship when I was on duty or speaking to a high-ranking officer. The fleet isn't exactly like Earth's military, but it's kind of modeled after it."

"Fleet isn't military?"

"Kind of...but not. United Earth is in charge of both, but it's two different branches. I know how complicated that sounds. Fleet handles the colonies, stations, and aliens, if there's a conflict. Military protects Earth, that solar system only, and the people living there."

"I understand. We have something like that. Fighters who choose to defend only our people and planet, and some who battle by hiring their services out to good causes."

"But you're a trader, right? You fought those Ke'ters as if you were military."

"Most Veslors are trained to fight. Some do it for pay. I prefer to trade to earn a living."

"What do you trade? If I may ask."

"You can ask me anything, Vivian. I mentioned the food-growing colonies. We mainly provide food and medicines to others. The planets in our system are good for growing things. Our people never go hungry, but it's not the same for other races." He smiled. "Our supply shuttles never run late. It's a matter of great pride."

"I'm sure my people could learn a lot from yours."

He nodded. "You need rest, Vivian."

She *was* tired. "I don't want to take your bed."

"I insist."

She reluctantly nodded. "Thank you."

He rose to his feet and offered his hand. His skin felt like velvet wrapped around strong bones. He pulled her to her feet and led her to the door on the left. It automatically slid open.

"Motion sensors?"

"Yes."

The bedroom wasn't large, and most of the space was taken up by a massive bed. The size of it shocked her a little. It had to be nine feet long, ten feet across. There was storage built into one of the walls.

"Be comfortable. The bathroom is next door. I'm sorry the rooms aren't connected."

She turned around, peering up at him. "I don't have any spare clothes."

He inched around her and touched a panel. A drawer slid out. "Search around. Use whatever you think will work. What is mine, we'll share. We'll be stopping at a colony in eleven days, and I'd be happy to buy you clothing that will fit there."

"That's too much, Brassi."

He closed the drawer and approached her, stopping with barely a foot of space between them. His gaze was kind. "No, it's not, Vivian. I would give you anything. I'll be here when you wake."

He left and the door closed, leaving her alone.

Vivian removed her shoes and socks, then stripped out of the oversized uniform. She kept on her sports bra and panties, climbing under the thick covers to find soft sheets waiting. The bed was huge and really comfortable, and she was exhausted. The little rest she'd gotten since the attack hadn't been more than a few hours at a time.

Brassi called his brother. "She's sleeping. Tell me true. Is she well?"

"I've gone over her scans. The female is fine. Elevated levels of stress showed but that's normal."

"Good."

"I can't tell you if she's breeding compatible with our kind. I'd have to run more tests."

He scowled. "I didn't ask that."

"I'm not blind, brother. You're attracted to the female. You risked our lives to help her."

"Our king wants better trade with Earthlings."

"That excuses the first time we helped...but you went back for her."

"It was the right thing to do."

Vassi paused before continuing. "You want the female."

Brassi sighed, deciding there was no reason to lie. "I do."

"She might not be able to bear your young. What then?"

Brassi considered it. "Everything about her draws me unlike any other female. Her scent. Her voice. I wish to touch her."

"Perhaps it's temporary."

"Doubtful," he admitted. "Both sides of me are lured by her."

"You're certain?"

"I feel calm when I'm near her."

"What if she can't breed your young?"

"It won't matter." He didn't want to think about that. "I will be sad, but not enough to regret it if she is mine."

"She's so small and strange."

Brassi snarled in warning.

"I'm not insulting your female, brother. I'm stating facts. It may not even be possible for you to copulate with her. You should discover if you're compatible before you settle your heart on her. Imagine locking yourself to a female without that kind of connection. It would destroy *both* sides of you. I never want to be the one to have to put you down if you go feral."

Brassi stared at the closed bedroom door. "She needs more time."

141

"But that's not how we are. Connections are made quickly. Find out now, or put her in the medical bay to distance yourself from her. She can be comfortable there until we reach someplace where she'd be safe to leave behind."

"Some of her own people want to kill her, Vassi."

"She'll be the death of *you* if you lock on to the female and it's not possible for you to copulate. I depend on you, brother. We all depend on you. We're a bonded grouping. Your loss would devastate us all. Go to the female, explain, and discover if you're compatible. All of our futures hang in the balance of everything you do."

Brassi ended the call and paced his living space.

He was a Veslor. Vivian was not. Her people didn't take mates. They made contracts.

He grimaced, disgusted by the concept. It sounded cold and impersonal. Would he be too much for the female? Too intense? What if she couldn't handle him?

He growled low and rubbed his chest when he felt his inner beast clawing at him. "Easy, my other half. I want her, too. We agree on this."

He stopped pacing, staring at the bedroom doors.

"We need to take the risk."

He decided to eat before waking Vivian. She needed rest. He could give her at least a few hours.

Chapter Ten

A large, warm hand rubbed her back. Vivian groaned in pleasure, the massage feeling incredibly good.

Then she remembered where she was and gasped, sitting up.

She turned to find Brassi sitting on the edge of the bed. His upper half was bare, but he still wore black pants. He was a handsome alien beast man. There was no denying it. Her attention dropped to his muscular arms and chest.

He was a big, fit alien beast man, too.

"Hi." She reached up and tried to finger-comb her hair. It was probably a mess. "Is it morning?"

He shook his head. "You've slept for four hours. I ate, trained with my brother, and then showered to give you more time. But now we must talk. There is an important choice you must make soon."

She was intrigued. "Okay. What is it?"

"You're aware I'm a Veslor. I'm greatly attracted to you, Vivian. *Both sides of me are...*"

She adjusted her position, angling toward him and keeping the blankets up to her chest, taking in what he'd said. "I don't understand. I mean, the attraction part I get. I'm attracted to you, too," she said, deciding he deserved her honesty. "But what do you mean by both sides? Is this something to do with you being a shifter?"

He smiled. "You're aware of that?"

"Somewhat. We were given some reports about Veslors, but not much information is available. The cultural department wanted to send a specialist out to the ninth quadrant to learn more about your people. Getting permission from United Earth takes time. From what some humans reported, you can change forms, but they never said into what."

Then his smile faded, and his golden eyes flashed with an emotion she translated as worry. "I will show you. You need to see both sides of me to make a decision."

Excitement filled her. "Really? It's not a secret with your people? There's a theory, that it might be something you don't show other races."

"Other races normally only see our animal side during battle."

That unsettled her a bit. "Okay. Why?"

"You need to see to understand. I showed you my claws. That's just a small part of my other half. It's...assertive."

She frowned.

"Aggression and rage are contained in one side of us. To fight, to defend, we let that side out. Our other side. Other half."

She didn't like the sound of that. "Will you be putting me in danger to show me?"

He smiled. "No. I could never hurt you, Vivian. Both sides of me want to keep you safe."

He'd saved her life, twice. Once by taking care of the Ke'ters and again when he'd picked her up in space. She nodded. "I trust you, Brassi."

"Good." He hesitated. "I need to let my more aggressive emotions rise to show you. They are not directed at you." He slid off the bed and stood, reaching for the waist of his pants.

She watched in stunned fascination as he bent, slowly shoving them down. When he straightened, she forced her gaze to lock on to his face as he stood before her naked. It was tempting to peek lower but she didn't have worry about fighting it for long.

Suddenly he bent again, a low snarl tearing from him.

Goose bumps rose along her arms at the animalistic sound, but she remained still. She had to believe Brassi wouldn't hurt her.

It happened fast. He went from being a man to something that resembled a panther from Earth—if it were dark gray, bigger, scarier, and almost human-looking in its facial appearance.

He climbed onto the end of the bed, standing on all fours, his golden eyes watching her.

She examined him back, from his big paws with razor-sharp claws, to his thickly muscled limbs, to the broad chest and torso. He had a small tail that whipped back and forth. His teeth were longer now than in his other form, and she was pretty sure he could rip her to shreds if he wanted to. His eyes, though, were the same as Brassi's as he studied her, as well.

She shoved the covers down and slowly got to her knees. "Can you understand me?"

He gave a small nod of his massive head.

"Can I touch you?"

He lowered to his stomach, sprawling on the bed.

Her hand trembled as she reached out. He had to weigh four hundred pounds, at least, and was way bigger than her. Her fingertips brushed his side. The velvety softness was gone from his dark skin; instead he felt smooth but tough.

"That's amazing!"

He flicked his tail, and then, just as swiftly, shifted back into his man form. She jerked her hand back and watched him stretch his body on the bed. He stayed on his stomach though.

She glanced at his ass; she couldn't resist. It was muscled and beefy, and looked human in appearance. The tail had disappeared.

Vivian let out a breath as she collapsed onto her butt.

"We're deadlier in that form while fighting. Harder to hurt."

"I can understand that. Can you shift if you're not feeling angry?"

"It's triggered by aggressive hormones."

She took that for a no. "Can you control your shifts? I mean, of course you can. You just did. What I mean is, if you're talking to someone and they make you angry, do you just shift, or is it something done at your will?"

He smiled. "It's never accidental. We learn control fast when we're very young."

That was fascinating. "You said I needed to make a choice. What does this have to do with it?"

He held her gaze. "My kind take mates."

"You told me that before." Her heart began to pound. She wasn't an idiot. He was talking about mating, something about a choice. He needed to tell her more before she assumed anything. It could be a mistake to jump to conclusions, but part of her couldn't help linking the two of them together.

Was he about to ask her if she wanted to mate with him? The concept was scary. They barely knew each other.

"I'm drawn to you, Vivian. Both sides of me are. As a Veslor, I lock on to a female and take her as my mate. I don't know if we're compatible...but I want to find out if we are. I showed you both sides of me because we're an emotional race. We not only live by our emotions, but they rule our bodies."

She was speechless, unsure what to say. Lots of questions filled her head.

"I'm locking on to you. It's pure instinct and emotion. It means I'm drawn to you strongly. Everything about you appeals to me."

"We just met," she blurted.

"That's how it is for Veslors. We feel intense attraction, and it only grows until we fully lock on to a female and claim her." He searched her eyes with his. "There are no contracts. Just need and desire. I want you, Vivian. Will you allow me to touch you?"

"Holy shit. You're serious, aren't you?"

He nodded. "I know we're different but it doesn't matter to me." His gaze lowered to her sports bra, and a low growl came from him. "I long to touch you. Taste you. Copulate with you. Claim you...keep you."

Her heart pounded faster, and she felt her body responding to his husky, raspy voice. The way he looked at her made her feel warm all over. "I need a shower."

His eyes widened. She'd surprised him. Herself, too.

"I'll be back." She shoved off the covers, scrambled off the big bed, and almost ran out of the room and into the bathroom. It was cowardly to flee, but she couldn't help it. Everything was happening so fast.

There wasn't a lock on the door. She stripped out of her sports bra and panties, then figured out how to use the odd shower. They used water aboard the ship. It wasn't exactly hot, more like tepid. She stood under it, trying to slow her heart, which proved difficult when her thoughts remained on Brassi.

He wanted to have sex with her! She wasn't even sure if that was possible. They were two different races. He was so much bigger than her. She should have peeked at his groin when he'd stripped, to discover what he had going on down there.

She opened a container on the shelf and sniffed the contents. Berries of some sort. She wasn't sure if it was body wash or shampoo. It didn't matter. She poured some into her palm, using it to scrub both her hair and skin. Then she rinsed and used the water to cleanse her mouth as best she could. She longed for a toothbrush.

She turned off the water and used a towel to dry, thankful Brassi hadn't barged into the bathroom.

He wanted to mate with her. Make her his. It was crazy. They didn't know each other well enough to make a lifelong commitment.

Then again, she had learned a lot about alien cultures. She knew mating practices varied widely.

The Crezzi were instantly drawn to their mates. They formed bonds for life without even speaking a word to their intended first. It was scent and visual attraction that brought them together. Then they bred eggs, dozens of them, and raised the young together. The Richlings took multiple breeding partners, never forming an emotional bond with anyone but their offspring. Their people were sexually attracted to each other based on strength. The weaker-born of their species never bred. They were turned into something similar to slaves, serving the breeders.

"Shit." She stared at the door, apprehension filling her. "I can't hide in here forever. *Think*, Vivian."

If Veslors were motivated by emotion when choosing their mates, she closed her eyes, trying to be the exact opposite. Rational. She'd been trained to assess other races and to be open-minded. It was her job. Never once, though, did she consider she might be asked to become some alien's mate.

Brassi wasn't just some strange alien, however.

She opened her eyes. No. Brassi was the guy who'd saved her life and fought the Ke'ters to protect her people. He'd flown his ship back to rescue her when he'd learned Commander Alderson planned to murder her.

And Brassi was someone she was definitely attracted to, even though he was very different from her kind.

"Shit." She took some deep breaths and walked to the door. "I'm not a coward."

The door opened, and Brassi stood in the living room. He had put his black pants back on, and he stopped pacing to stare at her.

"I frightened you. Apologies, Vivian. I didn't mean to provoke that reaction."

"I wasn't afraid. More overwhelmed. We're very different, Brassi. Humans do this thing called dating, where we spend time together, slowly getting to know each other. We sometimes spend years dating before deciding to get married."

"Years?" He looked shocked, and sounded even more so.

She nodded. "The shortest span I've personally ever known was a month. A couple I know met and married that fast. Then again, they worked on the same team and were basically spending all their time together. After a month, they decided to make it legal. I think mostly they decided to marry because one of them was being reassigned to another fleet ship. They weren't civilians. Fleet workers go where they're told and aren't given an option to say no. The couple didn't want to be separated, and there's a clause in fleet contracts that states married couples have the right to be kept together. The contracts ensure they work for the fleet for years at a time, and until that ends, the fleet kind of owns them."

"Slavery?"

"We don't use that term. The fleet pays for their training, invests time and money into their education for various jobs. For that opportunity, people agree that the tradeoff is worth it. Once they do their time, they can leave the fleet to work for someone else. Most just resign another contract and stay, since it's job security."

"What about you? Does the fleet own your time?"

She shook her head. "No. It's one of the reasons I decided to be a civilian worker. I paid for my own schooling with money that my father left me when he died. I wanted my choices to be my own."

Brassi walked closer to her, stopped feet away and held her gaze. "What is your choice, Vivian? Should I ask you to sleep in the medical bay to keep space between us, or will you remain with me? As I've said, I'm already locking on to you."

She bit her lip and tried to think. "What happens when you lock on?"

"I won't be able to let you go. You'll be mine. I'll be yours. We mate for life."

"I don't even know if we're sexually compatible."

"We could find out." His gaze traveled down her body. "What is Earthling foreplay? How do you arouse your kind?"

"Kissing. Touching. What about Veslors?"

"Females approach and become physically aggressive. If males aren't interested in kind, we'll snarl at them to warn them off. If we *are* interested, we wrestle and pin the females under us."

Her gaze traveled down his body. He was a massive alien beast man who looked positively dangerous. "Wow. Sounds violent." She hoped he didn't expect that from her. Her gaze returned to his. "You'd probably hurt me. I also can't imaging attacking you. I've only hit men that I didn't like, and I sure didn't want to have sex with them."

He nodded. "I don't want to hurt you, Vivian. I just want you under me."

"Then what?"

"To be inside you."

She hesitated. "I don't know if our, um...parts, will match up. I'm curious to find out, because I'm attracted to you. I'm just not sure about the mating part. Can we test whether or not sex is possible without locking?"

"Yes. I can copulate with a female without mating her."

"What's the difference?"

"It's hormonal."

"Like with your shifting?"

He nodded. "I can't mate if I stay in this form."

She felt the blood drain from her face. "You mean you shift to mate? That we'd have to bond while you're in your other form?"

"Usually. But you're not Veslor, and you can't shift forms the way our females do. It's something we'll have to figure out. I can tell by your fear that you wouldn't welcome me shifting to secure a mate bond with you that way."

She felt more than a little overwhelmed. "We have a word for that. Bestiality. It's...um...illegal."

"I don't understand."

"It's illegal for humans to have sex with..." She didn't want to insult him by calling his other form an animal. He wasn't one, despite what he could turn into.

"Aliens? Other races?"

"Something like that."

"Your people also want to kill you."

"Some of them. Not all."

He cocked his head, his golden gaze piercing. "Earthling laws don't matter here. We're on a Veslor ship. Under our laws, mating is natural and encouraged if we're fortunate enough to find our mate. Race doesn't matter to our king. You'll be considered Veslor once we bond. Your people can't arrest you. I wouldn't allow them to."

That might be a good thing, if Abby failed and Commander Alderson got away with his scheme. Her reputation and name could be smeared beyond saving, and United Earth would put out an arrest warrant for her. She'd be lucky if she only spent the rest of her life in prison. Worst case, they'd execute her.

The Veslors weren't allied with UE. It meant they were under no obligation to turn over a human to her planet.

That wasn't a reason to say yes. She felt guilty for even *thinking* about that being a reason why she'd consider becoming his mate.

She stared into Brassi's golden eyes and shoved all thoughts out of her head. Instead trying to focus on how she felt. The attraction was mutual. She stepped closer, wanting to touch him. Since he wanted her as well, there was no reason not to.

She lifted her hands and placed them on his velvety chest, loving how soft his skin was under her fingertips and palms. He was so firm. Muscled. Strong. Warm.

His nostrils flared and a low growl came from him. It wasn't scary, but sexy. He reached for her, too, putting his big hands on her towel-covered waist. "Yes?"

She found herself nodding. "We'll just take things slow, okay?"

"Yes."

They stood there, and she realized he seemed to be waiting for her to do something, to initiate the intimacy. "We should go into the bedroom."

He gave a sharp nod.

She backed up and let her hands slide off his chest. He released her hips, and her heart pounded once more as she turned, leading him into his bedroom. She reached for the towel and swallowed hard, tugging at the material where she'd tucked it into itself. It dropped slowly down her body.

Not daring to look back to see his reaction to her naked backside, she climbed up onto his bed and rolled over, lying flat on her back.

Vivian looked at his eyes to find him taking in every inch of her body. She felt heat flush her cheeks but she pushed her shyness back. "Am I anything at all like a Veslor female?"

He shook his head, his attention locked on her breasts. Brassi just stood there, mute, staring at her.

She inwardly cringed and sat up, resisting the urge to hide. "Am I unappealing naked?"

His gaze jerked to hers, and he made a soft, strange noise before speaking. "Not unappealing. I'm afraid I'll hurt you. Your skin looks extremely soft all over."

She wondered if soft meant squishy. Was he calling her chubby? She wasn't one to work out, and aside from Big M making her learn to defend herself, she wasn't exactly the physical type.

Her gaze darted to his arms, chest, and stomach. Brassi didn't seem to have an ounce of flab on him. He was all muscle and tight, dark skin.

Don't panic. Misunderstandings happen when two alien races talk, she mentally reminded herself. "Should I get dressed?"

"NO!"

Chapter Eleven

Vivian jumped over the loud snarl.

Brassi dropped to his knees. "Apologies! Don't fear me. I just worry I'll hurt you. You appear so fragile." He lifted his hands toward her, showing off his fingernails. They weren't claws at the moment, but he did have some thick, sharp-looking nails.

"You won't." She gave him a small smile. "We're going to take things slow, remember? Let's start with how I'm different. What are your females' bodies like, besides the fact that our skin textures are different?"

His gaze lowered to her breasts, and he touched the flat disks on his own chest. "Yours are larger and seem delicate."

She glanced at her breasts and reached up, cupping them, giving each one a good squeeze to demonstrate. "They won't fall off." Her smile that time was wider.

He growled low. "The centers are stiffening."

He was talking about her nipples. "That happens when they're caressed, or if it's cold."

"Does it hurt?"

She shook her head. "No." She pinched one to show him. The nipple tightened even more. "It feels good for most females, actually. As long as it's not too rough or the skin isn't broken, it's pleasurable."

He walked on his knees to the end of the bed but paused there, placing his hands on the mattress. She studied his features. He didn't look disgusted, just intensely curious.

She released her breasts and grew bolder, spreading her legs and pulling her knees up. His gaze lowered, and another low growl came from him, even sexier than the last

"How about here?" She lay back a bit, using her elbows to hold herself up so she could watch him. Next, she put her feet flat on his bed, lifting her hips a little as she spread her legs wider. It was brazen to show him her pussy, but it was the quickest way to learn about each other. She was all for that. "Are humans much different from Veslor females here?"

He nodded. "You're pink. Our females are dark." He lifted his body, crawling onto the bed.

She held still as he drew closer. The bed dipped, and she had to tense her abs to keep from being knocked flat. Brassi lay on his stomach as he inched between her spread thighs. She had to part them even more. He was a huge guy with wide shoulders.

He scooted up until his face was directly over her sex. He didn't look at her face, too intent on staring at that most delicate part of her. He adjusted and reached one hand toward her.

She relaxed as his velvety hand stroked her inner thigh.

"So soft," he growled.

"So are you."

That caused his head to jerk up, and his eyes widened.

She smiled. "You feel good to me. Your skin."

He inhaled. "And you smell nice...but not needy. How do I change your scent? Do you become oiled when you are ready to copulate?"

Oiled? She thought about that a moment. "I get wet. Yes." She pulled her arms out from under her, reclined fully, and smiled. "Okay. Human woman sex lesson." She looked down at him. "Ready to learn?"

"Yes."

"I've never touched myself with someone watching before, but I know I learn faster if I see how something's done. I'll show you what makes me wet, and my scent will probably change. Actually, I'm sure it will. I know your sense of smell must be way better than mine, and even I can pick it up when I'm turned on."

"Show me."

His voice had come out deeper, and she liked how gruff it sounded. Maybe that was a sign of *him* being turned on. He sure didn't seem turned *off* by her. That was a relief.

She touched her breasts again. "They're sensitive. Basically, most parts of me are with the right touch." She slid her hands down her ribs, over her stomach, and stopped her pussy. She hesitated, reached up, and wet one of her fingers by licking it. "Dry touching in this area isn't very comfortable. This helps." She reached back down and gently touched her clit. "This is *extremely* sensitive, and will turn me on super-fast. It's also how I get off."

"Get off?" He was growling his words now.

"Climax. Come. Um...how we complete sex."

"Show me," he urged again.

She began to rub her clit. He watched her finger, and she watched him. He licked his lips, the sight of his dark tongue making her wonder what it would feel like if *that* was on her clit, instead of her finger.

She spread her legs wider, pleasure tingling through her as her clit began to swell. It was the first time she'd ever played with herself in front of someone, and there was something really hot about it.

He made a low rumbling noise and lowered his face even closer. She could feel his hot breath on her. The rumbling grew louder, almost like purring. She hoped that was a good thing. His eyes seemed brighter, even as they narrowed. She also noticed his body tensing, the muscles on his arms bunching.

She moved her finger off her clit, going lower, feeling how wet she was becoming. Maybe that was why he was responding that way. She was definitely getting "oiled" for him.

He suddenly gripped her wrist and pulled her hand away from her pussy. She was breathing harder and had almost been there, ready to come.

"What's wrong?"

He released her wrist, and she watched as he licked his thumb then lowered it. He brushed it over her clit. It was much rougher textured than her own fingertip, but it didn't hurt. He was gentle as he began to rub.

She moaned, her muscles clenching.

He looked up, their gazes locking. He continued to rub.

"Just like that," she managed to say.

He grew bolder, rubbing a little faster. She closed her eyes and panted.

Then he stopped, taking his thumb off her clit. She opened her eyes and lifted her head.

"I'm hurting for you," he rasped. "You're well oiled."

He wanted to fuck her.

She nodded, ready to see if that would work. She wanted him inside her. Already so close, he might even be able to get her off with penetration.

They'd work it out. She wanted him just as badly.

"Will it hurt you if I push into you here?" His thumb touched her again, running over the opening of her pussy. "You appear quite small."

"Women stretch. Why don't you show me what you have?"

He lifted to his knees on the bed and straightened. She swallowed hard as she looked down.

He still wore his black pants—but there was a large, thick bulge beneath them now, and the material didn't conceal much. He looked big, but the shape seemed in line with what human guys had.

He gripped the waist of his pants and shoved them down, exposing his penis.

It *was* human-like. Mostly. The top was thicker than the shaft, but not by much. It was as dark as the rest of him. There were thin ridges running along the length of his shaft, from just under the top down to the base, that she figured might be veins. It was angled outward while erect.

Her gaze looked lower, to his balls. He appeared to have only one—and there was something blocking it from clear sight.

She sat up and hesitated before reaching for him. She paused, glancing at his face. "May I touch you?"

He gave a sharp nod. His features looked tense. "Will we fit together?"

"You're big. Not a shock. We'll work it out. I mean, you look like a human. Only bigger." She ran her fingertips along the underside of his shaft, somewhat surprised. The texture wasn't like his velvety skin. Instead, it was more like leather. Smooth leather, but for those ridges. His cock twitched, and some clear fluid eased out of the tip. It wasn't a lot. Just a few drops. It ran down the crown of his shaft, to where she held him.

She touched it, rubbing it between her fingers. It felt like baby oil. It had a similar slick consistency.

Oil. Now she understood. It seemed Veslors created great lubrication for sex. She ran her fingertips lower, to the strange thing between his shaft and ball sac. It was bumpy, a solid protrusion, like cartilage covered in that leather texture.

"What's this?"

"My yunce. It protects my seed sac from damage. It's usually not swollen like that unless I'm about to copulate. There is another one on the backside."

She couldn't see it, but she ran her hand under his ball. He may have only one, but it was large, like the rest of him. She caressed it…

161

He sucked in a sharp breath.

Vivian froze, looking up at him.

"Extremely sensitive. It's never touched."

"Am I hurting you?" She thought she'd been gentle.

"No."

"Is it okay that I'm exploring?"

He gave another brief nod.

She kept her hand between his slightly parted thighs, lightly cupping his ball. It took up the entire palm and then some. It was soft, not leathery in texture like his penis. She could feel the other protrusion behind it, like the one in the front. "That's pretty cool."

"I need you, Vivian," he rasped. "Can we discuss my body further later? I need to be inside you. I hurt for you."

She pulled her hand away and noticed that his shaft was certainly oiled now. More of that clear fluid spilled from the tip of his cock, and the shaft on the underside was well coated.

"Yes."

"Turn around. We breed with the female facing away."

"Doggy style." It shouldn't have come as a shock. He was a shifter who turned into an alien panther, after all.

She backed away, got up on her knees and turned around. She dropped to all fours, spread her thighs, and prayed that he'd fit.

Brassi leaned forward, crawling over her, and she felt his stiff shaft brush against her inner thighs. She parted them wider. His breathing had increased. She realized this was the first time she'd ever had sex without kissing someone first...but they'd find out later if he liked that or not.

She felt a little fear, but pushed it down. Brassi wouldn't hurt her.

He moved closer, molding his upper body to her back, pressing their skin together. The velvet texture made her smile. He braced on one arm and reached up, cupping her breast. He explored it, giving it a gentle squeeze, then played with her nipple. She softly moaned. He was taking things slowly, carefully.

The rumbling sound he'd made earlier returned. His chest vibrated along her back. It was almost like getting a light massage. He adjusted his body and released her breast, running his hand over her side down to her hip. He moved his legs, the mattress dipping with his weight as he seemed to shift it more to one side then the other.

"Slow," he growled.

"Slow," she agreed.

Then she felt the thick tip of his cock rub against her pussy.

She was still wet. He was, too, with that clear substance his body created when he was turned on. He rubbed against her slit a few times and brushed her clit. She moaned and arched her back, pushing her ass higher. He seemed to like that, she guessed, when the rumbling noise and vibrations increased. Then he stopped right at the seam of her...and began to push.

Her body resisted a little. He was incredibly thick. He paused, his hand sliding around her stomach to hold her. Then he pushed again.

Vivian closed her eyes, forcing her body to relax as he breached her.

It was a tight fit, but her body gave, taking him. A deep snarl sounded close to her ear. He pushed in farther, paused, withdrew a little, and then pushed deeper once more.

He felt amazing. Vivian moaned.

He froze.

"Keep going! You're not hurting me."

"You're so tight...and soft inside, too."

She wasn't sure what "soft inside" meant in relation to what he was used to, but at that moment, she didn't care. He worked his way deeper inside her, and deeper still—and something brushed against her clit.

She jerked, startled.

He froze again. "Am I hurting you?"

"No. I think your...um...pence thing just touched me is all. I forgot about it."

"Yunce," he corrected. "Is it too rough against your tender flesh?"

"Move again, and let's see."

He did, and the yunce brushed up against her clit once more. Her eyes widened as he started to gently fuck her. The bumpy cartilage shield thing felt incredible against her clit. She moaned louder, clawing at the bed. It was marvelous. Everything about him being inside of her was nothing short of mind-blowing. "Oh god!"

He stilled yet again.

"Don't stop! You're all in, right?"

"Yes."

"Keep going, Brassi."

He began to fuck her again, still going slow. She clutched the bed sheets, whimpering. "We work," she panted, "really well together. Faster!"

His rumbling increased, the vibrations in his chest growing stronger. He did as she asked, fucking her faster and a little harder. The yunce was strumming her clit, he was pumping inside her, and the combination of the two had to be the best thing she'd ever felt in her life. It was intense. So much so, she came in blinding pleasure, yelling his name.

He snarled and fucked her harder then, for several long moments, until his body stiffened, the vibrations stilled, and she felt him coming inside her.

His body shivered over hers, and both of them were breathing hard. Warm liquid slid down her thighs when he gently eased his cock from her body and sprawled onto his side on the bed, reaching for her as he did. He pulled her close and wrapped his big body around her. They spooned as they caught their breath.

He nuzzled her cheek with his. "Be my mate, Vivian."

She turned her head, staring into his eyes. "Just like that?"

He nodded, his gaze intense. "We do work. So well."

She found herself smiling. "You might be mating yourself to a wanted criminal, if Abby isn't able to clear our names with all the evidence the commander is set on destroying."

"I know the truth. You saved your people. Your laws are stupid if they insist you did wrong. No one will *ever* take you from me."

She stared deeply into his eyes—and didn't think.

Emotions were what Brassi used to make his decisions. She would do the same. She felt safe in his arms, extremely sexually satisfied, and had no urge to get away from him. She liked being so close.

"Yes."

He grinned, flashing those scary teeth of his.

She turned toward him. He eased his hold on her and lay back. She crawled up him a little and got comfortable against his side, using his broad chest to rest her chin, gazing at him. "What exactly do we need to do to become mates?"

"What we just did...but I need to shift."

That killed her joy a little bit, trying to imagine that.

"I'm the same size down here." He lowered his hand, cupping his now soft shaft. "Just the rest of me changes. You could close your eyes."

Vivian had always been fascinated by other races. She'd gone to college to study them, and had chosen her profession because she was so interested in learning about aliens. It was easy to accept that Brassi looked different from her. They'd had sex, he'd saved her life, and she was naked in bed with him. Nothing about his current form turned her off.

The alien panther he'd shifted into hadn't hurt her—but did she want it on top of her? Having sex with her? That part was tough to imagine. "I don't suppose you have alien liquor, do you?"

"I don't understand."

"Stuff you drink that makes you a bit drunk?"

He frowned but gave a nod.

"Maybe you could give me a little, we could fool around, and when I'm on all fours, just don't tell me before you're about to shift...?"

"Is my other side unappealing to you?" A flash of hurt showed in his expression.

That hurt killed her. But they needed honesty in their relationship. That was too important. "No. It's a human thing. I accept your other side, Brassi...but do your people ever have sex with one of you shifted while the other is not?"

He hesitated. "No. That would be strange."

"That's where I'm at in my head, too. It would be strange. A little drink might help me feel more relaxed about the experience."

"I understand. I'll get you some quill to drink."

She assumed that was alien booze. "Compromises are important." She smiled and stroked his chest. The texture of his skin was something she'd never tire of. "Is this a one-time thing to form a mate relationship, or something I need to adjust to doing on a regular basis?"

"Me taking you while in my other form?"

"Yes."

"Only to mate, or if we wish to attempt to breed cubs."

She masked her features to hide her surprise. "Cubs?"

"Babies. I don't know if we're compatible for having young."

"There's a lot I need to learn about you. It's a good thing we'll be together for a long time. You said mates are for life, right?"

He nodded.

She smiled again and scooted up higher. "Can I teach you about kissing?"

"You can teach me anything, Vivian."

She drew closer and licked her lips. "We put our mouths together and explore each other with our tongues."

He smiled. "I know kissing. We call it tangling tongues."

"Veslors do that?"

"Yes. But I feared you'd be wary if I put my teeth that close to you."

"You can put your mouth anywhere you want on my body. I know you won't hurt me."

His hand skimmed down her back to her butt and cupped one cheek. Then his fingers slid between her legs and across her slit. "Even here?"

"Oh yes."

He grinned. "You smell good when you're oiled. I wanted to taste you."

It was her turn to shiver. "Let me shower, and then you can go for it. First, though, let's try kissing."

"What is your obsession with bathing?" He looked perplexed.

She laughed. "Most humans are really into being clean before sex."

"Each time?" He looked stunned. "That would mean we'll run out of water before we reach our next stop." He found her clit and rubbed one of his thick pads over it.

She spread her legs more and gasped. Brassi was a fast learner. He knew exactly how to touch her. Her clit was a little sensitive but she wasn't about to complain. He already knew how to touch her in just the right way. The few human men she'd been with in school hadn't bothered to learn that, and they were her own race.

"No, not every time...but I should get clean down there if you want to put your mouth in that area. I'm soaked from both of us."

"You're perfectly oiled for copulating."

She dug her fingernails into his chest when he kept rubbing against her clit, applying a little more pressure. "I can't think when you do that."

"Tongue tangle with me. I'll be careful not to hurt you."

She eased herself onto his broad chest and lowered her head, closing her eyes. Their mouths touched, and she opened hers, running her tongue along the seam of his lips. He groaned, opening to her.

Then he quickly took over, rolling and pinning her under him. He explored her mouth, deepening the kiss.

She moaned against his tongue and spread her legs, wrapping them around his hips. He was erect again. She could feel the thick hardness of him. She broke the kiss and opened her eyes. "Do you ever have sex in this position?"

He shook his head. "No, but I'll try it if you want."

"I want."

He adjusted his hips...and then he was pushing inside her. She moaned as he thrust deep. That vibration from his chest started again as he made rumbling noises. There was no yunce to rub against her clit in this position, but his body did that as he angled his pelvis and began to move over her, driving in and out of her body harder, faster.

"We *work*," he growled low, taking her mouth again and kissing her.

Chapter Twelve

Brassi strode into the common room where his males were eating dinner. They all paused, staring at him. He saw their nostrils flaring, and he grinned widely.

Vassi stood, food forgotten. His brother appeared anxious. "You copulated with her?"

"Many times."

"Should I take a look at her?"

"No! She's my female. You stay away." He walked over to a cupboard and yanked it open, moving bottles until he found some quill, and grabbed it. He turned to go back to his quarters, where Vivian waited.

Vassi had moved into his path. "She's much smaller than you. Are you sure you didn't do her any harm? I should run a medical scan to make certain."

"I wouldn't hurt my mate."

Vassi gasped. "You mated her?"

"I will." He showed him the quill. "She asked for a few drinks of this, since I need to change forms."

Ruggler got up from the table. "How did you convince her to copulate with you? Did she attack you?"

Brassi's shook his head. "I want to get back to her before she gets out of the shower."

"How do you copulate with her without doing harm? She seems so frail." This from Kavs.

He shot him a glare. "Carefully. With tenderness. But she's not as fragile as she looks." Then he glanced back at Ruggler. "And I asked. She agreed. No wrestling was involved. Their females aren't aggressive."

Vassi reached out and touched his arm, stilling him once more when he would have walked away. "You truly fit inside her? She looks small all over. You really should allow me to run a medical scan."

He glanced at his males. Their expressions were ones of curiosity and concern. He sucked in a breath and blew it out. These males were close to him, bonded, and they'd spent years together. He trusted them with his life, and in their place, he might also be worried and curious. He finally stared into his brother's eyes.

"The human females stretch inside to accommodate a male. I was gentle, and I fit easily. She's not harmed. I asked her. She initiated copulation the second and third time. Vivian wouldn't have done so if my size was uncomfortable for her." He turned to Ruggler. "Go on. Ask your questions. You always have the most."

Ruggler grinned. "Are they like our females?" He pointed at his lap.

"Different. Pink. Delicate, with a fleshy bump near where we enter them. It's extremely sensitive. She needs a light touch when I rub it, and it makes her well-oiled. And humans don't snarl in pleasure. Instead, she makes soft keening noises of encouragement." His chest puffed with pride. "Then she screams my name when I complete her." He reached up and rubbed one ear. "Pull away a bit when that happens. My ear is still ringing a little." He chuckled. "Though, I'm not complaining."

"What about how they feel?"

He knew Ruggler would ask that next. "Also different, but immensely pleasurable."

"How so?" That was Nessel. It was rare for him to care enough to ask anything. But at the moment, the male was watching him intently.

Brassi considered the question. "She's soft inside. Extremely tight, but soft." He touched his skin. "Not like our flesh; in a different way. I enjoyed being inside her so much, it was difficult for me to hold back from spilling until after she was completed. It's that pleasurable."

"Are we like their males?" Yoniv asked, getting another plate of food.

"Their males don't have a yunce. Vivian was very curious about that. She felt mine."

Vassi drew his attention by gasping. "You allowed her to touch you near your seed sac?"

"She has no claws. She wasn't going to accidently tear my sac. Their males don't have any protection there. And she enjoys them. The top one rubs against her fleshy sensitive part while I'm copulating with her. We tried one of her human positions, but she likes being taken from behind better. My yunce rubs up against her the most that way. Can I return to her now? I'll answer more of your questions later. I want to mate her."

"Why the quill?" Vassi released his arm.

He felt a little embarrassed by that. "This form is pleasing to her...but my battle form makes her nervous."

"It's still you," Nessel grumbled, looking offended.

"It is, but she made a good point. We don't copulate with our own females when they are in their battle form, and we're not. It would be strange. It's odd for her to think of me changing forms to copulate with her, when humans don't shift."

"Makes sense." Yoniv sat at the table again, digging into his food. "Did you tell her that part of your body will remain the same?"

Brassi nodded.

Vassi frowned. "We're not aware if they are breeding compatible. Are you certain you're willing to give up becoming a father if Vivian can't have your cubs?"

"She's mine. Copulating locked me to her. It was already difficult not to change forms, and I had to battle to keep control. She wanted some quill first."

"Scussusk," Nessel hissed.

Brassi shoved the bottle of quill at his brother, stomped over to the male, grabbed him, and yanked him out of his seat. He pinned him to the nearest bulkhead to snarl in his face.

Nessel opened his hands, not fighting back. "Not against your mate."

"Then why utter the curse?"

"You said copulating with the female locked you to her. Will that happen to any of our males? We lose the choice to walk away after copulating with a human?" He looked terrified at the idea. "Maybe these aliens can force us to lock on to them with their bodies."

He released Nessel and backed off. "I felt the pull before we copulated. I held back the urge, but being intimate with her broke my resolve to resist. Stop being so paranoid, Nessel."

"I will volunteer to find out," Kavs chuckled. "To see if copulating with one of these Earthling females causes us to mate them. Brassi looked well satisfied with the experience—until you infuriated him. I've never seen him happier than when he entered the room."

Nessel flashed his teeth, adjusted his clothing, and returned to his seat. "You would. Foolish."

Brassi took the bottle of quill from his brother and left the common room, hurrying back to his quarters. The door opened, and he spied Vivian already lying in their bed.

He'd changed the settings on the interior doors, and she liked to keep them open. *He* didn't, since she was currently nude, and anyone happening down the hallway might have glimpsed her as he entered. He rushed inside before anyone could come along. That sight was his alone.

"Is that your alien booze?"

He nodded, stopping at the side of the bed. "Are you certain you wish to try it? It's strong."

She sat up and reached for the bottle. "I'll take a drink and see how it goes." She accepted it, studying the lid.

"Twist."

She did, and opened it. "Do you have a glass?"

"We just drink from it."

"Shared bottle, huh? When in Rome."

"What does that mean?"

"It's a saying that means to do something that others are doing; that it's fine even if it's different from what you're used to." She smiled and put the lip of the bottle to her mouth, taking a sip. She lowered it fast and gasped, her eyes widening. She blew out a sharp breath. "Wow. That's got a kick. It's burning all the way down to my belly."

He snatched the bottle from her, concerned. "It's hurting you? I'll get Vassi!"

She grabbed his wrist. "I'm *fine*. It's just an expression. I'm not really burning."

He refused to give her the bottle again. "Our females don't drink quill. Maybe you shouldn't, either."

She hesitated but then handled over the lid. "Maybe not." Her eyes looked watery.

"Let me call Vassi."

"No. I'm good. That stuff is just strong. How much can you drink?" Her gaze darted up and down his body. "Probably all of it."

He put the lid on the quill and sat it on the table next to his bed. "No. Just a few swallows. Quill is potent. One bottle lasts our males quite a while."

"When do you drink?"

"For celebrations, like when we make a very profitable trade. We all took drinks when we returned from your vessel after fighting the Ke'ters. None of us were injured. It was a good day. It's tradition with our males. Everyone will drink once we mate."

She smiled. "That's kinda sweet. Your crew will want to celebrate that?"

"I'll be the first one of us to mate. We all wish to find a female to claim. And I've found you." He sat at the edge of the bed and took her hand.

"Do they know that we're going to become mates?"

"Yes. I told them."

"How did they take it? Were they shocked or upset because I'm not a Veslor?"

"No." He decided to confess something to her. "Remember when sometimes we'd switch languages on your vessel? They were teasing me about my strong attraction to you, and giving me tips on how to gain your interest in return."

She didn't look angry. Instead, she smiled. "Really?"

He nodded. "They are happy for us. Curious, too."

"I bet they are. I totally understand. I mean, I selected my profession because of my curiosity about alien races and the differences between us. I've always been fascinated by the unknown."

"Are you ready to find out how mating is done?"

"I'm still nervous...but I want to do this with you. That quill stuff is already working. I feel a little tipsy."

"What is that?"

"A good thing. A little drunk. Not too much, but relaxed. It did what it was supposed to do."

He stood and shoved down his pants, the only clothing he wore. His gaze darted around the room, and he grabbed pillows he kept on a low bench along one wall. He dropped them on the floor near the end of the bed.

Vivian rose up to her hands and knees, crawling toward him. "What are you doing?"

"We have no breeding benches onboard."

"What's that?"

He looked at her—and chuckled. Her face had paled. "Nothing bad. It's an easier way for us to copulate in battle form."

"But I can't shift."

"I know. That's why we'll use pillows. To cushion your softer body."

"Oh boy. This is going to be an experience, isn't it?"

He stilled, worried she might change her mind. "I won't hurt you, Vivian. You can trust me."

"I do. I said yes, remember?" She gave him a timid smile. "I'm fully committed to you...to this. Do you bite?"

He felt horrified. "No!"

She laughed. "Whew!" She wiped her forehead as she sat on her legs. "I'm glad to hear that."

"Why would you ask such a thing? That would hurt you." He opened his mouth to show off his teeth once more, in case she'd forgotten what they looked like.

"I read some books. Shifters who bite to claim their mates. Forget it."

"They sound like horror stories."

She laughed harder. "Maybe. Is mating a chemical thing? Or just symbolic?"

"It's physical." He tried to think of a way to explain it. "We shift forms, which you know."

"I do. It's pretty amazing."

"To mate, the male's body creates a special oil."

Her gaze dropped to his groin. "Oh. Okay." She stared into his eyes next. "Will this do anything to me physically?"

"You'll carry my scent, making all males aware that you are my mate. At least that happens to Veslor females. I'm not sure with you."

"I guess we'll find out soon enough if your sperm does something strange to me."

"Sperm?"

"Seed. I think that's the same in my language."

He nodded and dropped to his knees, stacking the pillows in two piles in front of him, leaving room in the middle for Vivian. He backed up and pointed. "You get on your hands and knees here."

"Why the pillow walls next to me?"

"When I shift forms, I don't want my claws to touch you. They will remind me not to grab hold of your body."

"Is that a worry?"

"I held you in place before."

"Right. You did. You seem to like to clutch me around my waist while we're going at it. I guess that would be bad if you had sharp claws."

He watched her get on her knees in front of him and bend over. His gaze locked on her pale ass. She had a nice one, soft yet firm, with plenty of padding. He enjoyed slamming his pelvis against her there. Veslor females had harder, more muscular bodies. He preferred Vivian's. He could feel his rod stiffening already, wanting to be inside her.

"Brace your arms on the end of the bed, on the metal holding the mattress in place."

She gripped the bar but then paused, looking back at him.

"Are you changing your mind?"

She shook her head. "No. I just think this might not work."

Disappointment flooded him. Vivian didn't want to mate him.

She got up, releasing the bar. "I'm just going over it in my head. I've seen you shifted... Follow me."

He stood, his rod stiff. She entered his living space and walked to one of the couches, where she lowered herself to bend over one end. Her upper body was on the padded material.

"How about this? When you shift, you'll be on all fours, and I'm kind of pinned against something solid. I won't have to try to brace myself with my arms, and you won't feel the need to hold me in place while you're doing me." She rocked her body to show him that she was pinned against the edge, firmly in place. "See? You said you have breeding benches. Is it to hold the female securely so you don't claw them?"

He grinned, feeling relieved. "Yes. You're a smart female, Vivian." He walked behind her, admiring her ass again, and then kneeled. It was a good height for him, but her knees didn't touch the floor. They hung inches above it. She wiggled a little farther up, getting more comfortable.

He moved into position behind her, noticing there was ample room on either side of her upper body for his limbs, once he changed. He licked his thumb and reached between her legs, finding her clit.

"I will get you well-oiled for me."

She spread her thighs apart. "You're really good at that." A soft moan came from her. "I love your calluses, or whatever that rougher texture is on the tips of your fingers."

He ran his other hand up her back, caressing her. He wished he could touch her breasts. They were soft as well, and he loved having them in his palms. She lay flat on his couch, though, making them unreachable. He focused on her fleshy tender bump instead, feeling it swell. Her oil came readily as he brushed against her slit.

She moaned and wiggled in front of him. He wanted her so badly, his rod hurt. Vivian had a shocking effect on him. No female had ever made him feel so needy. She became well-oiled, and he released her clit and drew closer. He guided the tip of his rod to her pussy, and he began to push inside. She whimpered as she took him.

He closed his eyes and felt his chest vibrate from the pleasure. She was hot, oiled, and perfect. It felt so good to be joined with her. He pushed in deeper, as he pinned her under his body. She moaned louder, making those keening noises he liked so much. He pushed all the way in and paused, then began pumping his hips in slow rolls.

He opened his eyes, watching as Vivian's small, blunt finger claws dug into the cushions. She frequently did that when he was giving her pleasure.

He pumped into her faster, and her keening increased in volume. Her soft interior squeezed around his rod, and he felt his aggression rising, the urge to mate overcoming him. This time he didn't resist, allowing his emotions free reign.

The shift happened fast, as it always did, and he battled a little for control. He wanted to take her hard and fast, but she was too delicate. He dropped his upper limbs next to her torso and pinned her tighter under him.

His female was taking his other form. His beast was inside her.

She kept keening, his name on her lips, and he nuzzled her head with his muzzle. He couldn't help it.

"Oh god, Brassi!" she cried out.

He felt her insides tighten to the point he had to fight to move, and he worried he'd hurt her, but she didn't buck to get free or otherwise struggle. Her hands opened and closed as she grabbed the cushions, clawing at them.

Brassi threw back his head and snarled as he found his release. It was strong enough to make him nearly collapse on her fully. He recovered fast, though, adjusting the weight of his battle side. He couldn't shift back yet. He felt too drained.

He panted hard. So did Vivian.

Vivian had a heavy beast on top of her.

She opened her eyes, glancing at his arm. It was more of a limb and a paw, with sharp claws. He'd really shifted while inside her. She'd kept her eyes closed after Brassi had entered her, and hadn't felt the change.

Not that she could think much at all when he fucked her. His yunce made sure of that. The stimulation of him thrusting inside her and having her clit manipulated at the same time made for extreme climaxes. Now she realized the skin pressed against her back felt different. Leather-like. She could feel a light sheen of sweat, too. Probably hers. She wasn't sure if Veslors sweat at all. He hadn't before. It was definitely her. He currently didn't have that velvety fur rubbing against her to wick away the moisture.

She felt surprising calm, despite knowing if she twisted her head to look at Brassi, he'd be all alien panther. It was still him. Sex had felt the same. He still vibrated and rumbled while fucking her. She reached out and hesitantly touched his paw.

The claws attached to it curled, digging into the cushion. She noticed then that it was ripped. That must have happened while they were going at it. Maybe having him take her on his couch wasn't a good idea after all.

She lowered her head and closed her eyes, catching her breath. A weird vibrating sensation came over her then. Vivian felt his body tremble, and the leather-like feel of him returned once more to velvet.

She opened her eyes—and stared at his hand and arm. He was back.

She twisted her head, staring at his face.

Their gazes locked, and she smiled. "The couch is toast, but I'm feeling great."

"Toast?"

She pointed at the tears. "Um, it got damaged. But I didn't. Are we officially mated now?"

He leaned in and brushed his lips over hers, kissing her. "Yes."

"How long before we know if I'm carrying your scent?"

"Hours. You can shower, and then I'll have Vassi smell you."

"You can't tell?"

"It's harder for me. We are adjusted to our own scents."

"That makes sense." She nodded.

He backed off, withdrawing his cock from her body. She hated that part. Their joined fluids leaked down her thighs every time. But he turned her on like crazy, and it seemed he came hard with her, as well. That made for a mess. She scooted backward a little and slid off the edge of the couch, her knees hitting the floor, then started to stand.

Brassi helped her, his hands gentle. Concern showed on his face when she looked up at him.

"I'm fine, Brassi."

"I worried I'd be too rough. I wasn't?"

"No. You felt a little heavier at the end, but that's all I noticed. And just barely. I told you that when you touch me, you make thinking hard. I really enjoy sex with you. It's the best thing ever."

"You kept your eyes closed."

She felt a little embarrassed now, considering there hadn't been anything to fear after all. "I won't next time."

His eyes widened.

She smiled and shrugged. "When in Rome. I was a little fearful, but there wasn't anything bad about what we just did. It was as wonderful as always."   .

"I'd only do that again if we wanted to breed a cub." He led her into the bedroom and steered them to the bed. He lay down and opened his arms.

She climbed in after him and snuggled close. Brassi liked to hold her, and she liked being held *by* him. She rubbed her cheek against his silky chest and smiled. "I love that you cuddle."

"It's bonding. Mates do this."

"You liked to hold me before we'd officially mated."

"I knew you were mine from the start."

Her smile grew wider. "We feel right together."

He nuzzled the top of her head with his jaw. "We fit perfectly."

"We do." She yawned. "I could go for a nap. I don't even know what time it is."

"You need sleep, but you should eat first."

"Later. Right now, I just want to sleep with you."

He ran his hand over her back, caressing her. "We'll eat later. It's been a full day for us both."

"It has." She kissed his chest and closed her eyes, yawning again. "Good night, Brassi. Thank you for making me your mate."

"It's my honor, Vivian."

Chapter Thirteen

Vivian felt a bit shy three days later, when she left Brassi's quarters with him for the first time. They'd spent the previous days alone, bonding. He'd left to get them food but always returned quickly. Now his crew wanted to see them both together, and she only hoped they would accept her as easily as Brassi had implied. Humans would have a much harder time with her mating to a Veslor. At least, she was pretty sure they would.

They entered what Brassi called the common room. The males were at a table with plates. Everyone stopped talking to stare at them. Vassi rose to his feet first and ran his gaze over her from head to foot.

"Hello, Vivian. How are you?"

"I'm great." She tightened her hold on Brassi's hand. Vassi was his brother, family. His reaction mattered the most to her.

The male came closer and his nostrils flared. He grinned, looking at his brother. "She carries your scent strongly."

"She does," one of the other men agreed. He peered at her with curiosity. "You both showered but your scent is strong. I no longer pick up her Earthling scent. Just yours."

"No copulation smells," another one muttered. "All Brassi. She's your mate. You did it. Scussusk."

Brassi snarled at him. "I warned you, Nessel."

Vivian glanced between the two. "What did he say? I really need to learn your language."

Vassi waved his hand. "It is a noise we make when we don't agree with something. It's not because you mated." He stepped closer. "We all are happy you are Brassi's mate. Nessel is unpleasant all the time about many things. He fears all Veslors will automatically mate to your females now, if we copulate with them."

She took that in, her mind working it over. "Oh." She forced herself to look at the upset Veslor. He was a handsome guy, despite the way he scowled...or what passed for one. "I see. That would be a problem, wouldn't it?"

Nessel's eyes narrowed.

"I mean, humans have sex with each other just for pleasure," she explained. "It would be scary if we mated accidentally all the time, instead of doing it intentionally."

"I volunteer to find out. Do you know any unmated Earthling females who will copulate with me?"

She jerked her attention to a smiling Veslor male. He was handsome, too. "Not really."

"What about that female you were speaking to on your vessel? The one in your ear."

"Abby. I don't know. Right now she's got other things to worry about." *Like staying alive and keeping Commander Alderson from destroying evidence.* Guilt hit next as she thought about the danger Abby could be in.

"Enough," Brassi snapped. "You're making my mate sad."

"I'm fine," she told him. "Abby's still on the *Gorison Traveler*. Has anyone heard from her?" She glanced around at Brassi's crew.

One of them shook his head. "Not since she asked us to come back for you." He paused. "I'm Kavs."

"Hi." Vivian waved to him. "It's nice to meet all of you, and thank you for rescuing me twice."

One of them chuckled. "I'm Ruggler. No thanks required. Brassi didn't want to leave you in the first place. He was happy when the call came and eager to get you back and on our ship."

Another male snickered. "Eager to get her under him and claim her as his mate."

"Yoniv," Brassi growled.

The male laughed. "Truth. You mated her." He winked at Vivian. "Welcome to the *Brar* and our family."

She took in their faces. Only Vassi and Brassi looked similar. "You're all related by blood?"

"No." Brassi led her to the table and helped her sit. "We grew up together though, like family. Our bond is strong." He left her to go get two plates of food from a serving counter.

Vassi sat across from her. "We form groupings."

"I'd love to hear more." She gave a thankful smile to Brassi as he sat a plate of meat, what looked like steamed rice, and some kind of purple veggies in front of her. He left again and came back with two cups of the berry-scented drink before sitting next to her.

"Groupings are tight relations with close friends who grow up together," Ruggler explained. "We choose to stay together throughout our lives."

"Work together. Live together," Nessel grumbled. "Even if we don't want to."

Some of the males chuckled. It was Brassi who spoke. "No one else wanted Nessel in their grouping. So we welcomed him into ours."

The male made a low rumble sound but that was it.

Vassi met her gaze. "He's got an unpleasant outlook on most things. It annoys many. We're used to it. He's family in our minds."

She nodded. "What happens if someone doesn't have a grouping to belong to?"

Brassi stiffened slightly.

She looked at him. "Was that offensive to ask? I'm sorry."

"It's a sad thing," Ruggler replied. "The males and females don't survive long on their own." He touched his chest. "Alone, we're empty inside. Veslors are built to be together in groups. It also offers protection. We fight together. Watch out for each other. Care for our grouping."

All the males nodded, even Nessel.

"I like that." Veslor groupings sounded nice to her.

Ruggler leaned closer. "Humans don't have this?"

She shook her head. "Not really. We have family and good friends but we don't stay together from childhood to the end of our lives. Only couples stay together once they're married, but not always for the rest of their adult lives."

"Married?" Kavs asked.

"Mated. But if it doesn't work out, they divorce. My parents did that."

"What is that?" Nessel stared at her intently.

"Nothing you need to know," Brassi grumbled. "You'll just worry Vivian will leave me. But she won't."

"He'll die if you leave him!" Nessel shot to his feet, knocking over his drink, and snarled at her. "You can't do that."

Brassi stood and snarled back. "Don't talk to my mate with that tone!"

"Whoa!" Vivian stood, too. "I'm never leaving Brassi. Please don't fight." She glanced at them, then the others. "There's a lot we need to learn about each other. I accept Veslor mating rules and swear to never leave Brassi. I'm with him for life."

"It's not a rule." Vassi spoke quietly. "We mate for life, but if our mate dies or leaves, we give up living...or wish we had." He glanced at Nessel, then gave Vivian a telling look. "The males change inside. Lose their heart if they survive the loss of a mate."

Vivian sat down. "I see." She looked at Nessel, feeling sad for him, pretty sure Vassi was trying to convey that's what had happened to his friend. She totally understood his worry for Brassi if that was true. "I'm never going to leave Brassi. I promise, Nessel."

He sat, appearing calmer. "Good."

They resumed eating after the spilled drink was cleaned up by Yoniv, the silence unnerving. She took a sip of her drink and cleared her throat. "Is there anything you want to know about humans?"

"You don't want to offer that," Brassi warned. "They will ask about copulating. Your face turns pink sometimes with *me*, and I'm your mate."

She laughed. "True, but I'm sure they're curious. I became a cultural specialist because of my curiosity about other races. Now I'm living on your ship. I'm sure there're things they'd like to know about me and my kind. It's okay. This is how we can learn about each other. Part of my alien studies had some anatomy lessons that I found fascinating. For instance, the Crezzi have a ball-like penis that pushes out of their lower stomachs, where it's usually hidden until breeding. They don't just ejaculate their sperm—um...seed—from one hole, but a dozen of them on the rounded surface of their sex organ. And the Bri have two penises that look like twisted rods. I can talk about this stuff."

Brassi shot a warning look at his males. "Keep it polite." Then he waved his hand, as if they could start.

Kavs was first. "How do your females let a male know if they want to copulate?"

"See?" Brassi sighed.

She just smiled and took a deep breath. "We flirt and then date." She went on to explain further, and their reactions had her laughing. They were mostly horrified.

It was a pleasant meal after that. She liked answering their questions, even if some of them were very personal, including about her own body parts and explaining human male anatomy.

190

When they finished eating, they moved to couches around the room, just hanging out together. Brassi stayed at her side, holding her hand the entire time.

"You should make detailed announcements to share with our males," Ruggler suggested.

Vivian cocked her head. "Announcements?"

"Written documents for them to read. Many males will be curious once they learn Brassi mated an Earthling female. Especially undesirable ones like us, who have little chance of finding a mate of our own kind."

That confused her. "Undesirable?"

"Females want to stay with their own groupings on our home world. They don't like to live on ships." He motioned around the room. "Space travel is not an interest to them. Any male who doesn't live on a planet full time is undesirable as a mate. But you give us hope we can still find mates. You're copulation compatible with Brassi."

Kavs vigorously nodded. "Our females also don't prefer males with groupings this large. They like to bring those males into their female groupings. At six, we stand no chance."

"What does that matter?"

The males glanced at each other. Was there something Brassi hadn't told her about becoming his mate?

A horrible suspicion built...and she felt the blood drain from her face. She stared at Brassi.

Did *groupings* mean they shared their females with the other men?

That wasn't going to happen. No way, no how, would she ever let them pass her around.

Brassi frowned, watching her. "What's wrong?"

"Why do your females not like male groupings?"

Ruggler touched her leg and she jumped, jerking away.

He frowned, letting her go. "It's the living situation. Groupings stay together. We share this ship, and it's not large. We'd have to buy a larger ship if each of our mates had groupings, to fit them here—if they consented to live on a ship at all. Smaller groupings are better when mating. On our planet, it would mean building onto their homes to make room for more to live together. It can get expensive. You look frightened, Vivian. Why?"

Brassi's eyes narrowed...and then he growled. "We don't share mates. Is that what you thought?"

She relaxed. "Maybe. How did you guess?"

"You were looking at my males with fear and flinched when Ruggler gained your attention with touch. I'd kill one of them if they tried to copulate with you. Our females just don't like having to live with dozens of people in their homes. It can get that way quickly, once the mates breed cubs. Some homes have over fifty living together."

She snuggled against him. "Sorry. We have a lot to learn about each other still. No offense to anyone, but I'm glad to hear I'm just yours." She gave the other guys a shrug. "Most humans, at least this one, are into being with just one person. Not, um, groups for having sex."

Nessel let out one of his already familiar low growls. "She'll want you to herself, then—and ask you to leave us."

Vivian met his gaze. "No. I understand. We're a family and will live together. I'm fine with that. When each of you finds a mate, it will mean I have females to make friends with. Humans just tend to come alone if you mate with one of them. No groupings to find rooms for."

Nessel snorted. "*Now* she will urge us all to mate with her kind. I'm not taking one."

Kavs chuckled. "Her females will be grateful for that."

* * * * *

Brassi was glad Vivian had been accepted by his males. Only Nessel had any problems with their mating, but that particular male worried about everything.

He took Vivian to their quarters and sealed them inside. She turned to him. He spoke first. "I should have explained groupings to you. I'm sorry. It's just how it's always been for us. I didn't consider how you'd feel, knowing the males on this ship are with us for life."

"I think it's great, Brassi."

"Even Nessel?"

She smiled. "He's a bit paranoid."

"He's had a hard life."

She pulled him by his hand to the couch and sat. "Tell me about him. I mean, if you can. I'd like to understand."

"His parents died when he was young. There was a storm while they were traveling. He was too young to go and remained with the rest of their grouping. Their deaths left him unhappy and desolate, and his grouping began to reject him for not being a playful cub. We lived close to his grouping, and saw him alone often."

Tears welled in her eyes. "How old was he?"

His mate was sensitive and caring. He liked that. "Three years. We drew him to us and made him one of ours. He wasn't playful but we included him in everything. He put up with us." He smiled at the memory of Nessel scowling at them all the time, refusing to play games, but he always stayed close. "By four, he had moved in with us. There was a female, though, from his first grouping, who he felt strong emotions for. He watched her from afar, always."

"His mate?"

Brassi touched his chest, and then his head. "In here, and here, but she wasn't interested in him. She never approached him when we grew older. Instead, she mated to someone else. He was deeply hurt. We thought we'd lose him. He didn't want to eat. Sometimes we'd make him."

She arched her eyebrows. "Literally?"

He chuckled. "Yes. We pinned him and wouldn't let him up until he ate. He got angry about that but it worked. Then we decided to become traders. It saved him from seeing the female with her mate every day, once we left our home world. We hoped he'd grow better. And he did." He hesitated. "I worry about how he'll take it, now that I'm mated. So far it's just been us males."

"Maybe we can find him a mate."

Brassi leaned closer to her and pressed a kiss on her lips. "You are a sweet one, Vivian. But no female would want to mate with him. He's grumpy and not pleasant. We make stops at our growing colonies often to pick up trading supplies. Some females there are unmated and will copulate with him. That's enough."

"Maybe one of them will want to mate someday."

He shook his head. "They have large groupings and don't want to leave their home planet. Our females really don't like traveling, and I'd worry if he ever left us. We look out for him. I don't think any other grouping would accept him. Males like us are only for copulating with. A temporary experience."

"Oh." She frowned.

"What is it?"

"Do you copulate with a lot of females?"

He hid a smile. His female was jealous. "You're it for me for life, Vivian. The only female I want to touch. Forget my past. I already have. You are my future."

"We haven't really talked about that stuff. Do you have any cubs? I should have asked that."

He shook his head. "Only mated couples have cubs."

"It never happens by accident?"

"No. Does that happen with humans if they aren't married?"

"All the time."

He was stunned.

She nodded. "We ovulate every month and can get pregnant if we don't use protection."

"What is that?"

"Protection? There are shots we take to avoid getting pregnant. Without them, our men can impregnate any female who is ovulating. Married or not."

"Are you on protection?"

She grinned. "No. I'm not on the shot. I wasn't dating anyone. No copulation for a long while."

He nodded. "Did you copulate often?"

She shook her head. "No. I grew up on the *Gorison Traveler*. Most of the guys assigned there aren't looking to get married. They just want to hook up with as many women as possible. Man whores aren't my thing."

"Man whores?"

She hesitated. "Guys who have sex with a lot of women, sometimes just to see how many they can get into bed. It means nothing to them. It's about numbers, not emotion. I had a few of them come after me because it was a big 'fuck you' to my dad. At least, I guessed that was their motivation. He was their boss. I didn't want to be a way for them to retaliate against him for whatever slight they felt he'd given them during work. It wasn't until I went to Earth that I felt any guys were interested in me for the right reasons, and had sex."

"Your people are strange."

"Yes. They can be."

"I should ask you if you've had cubs, since your kind can have them without being mated." He *definitely* felt jealousy. Had a male given her a cub when Brassi couldn't?

"No. I was really careful to avoid getting pregnant. I was on the shot while on Earth."

He breathed out in relief. "Good."

"I also wouldn't have left the *Gorison Traveler* without my child if I had one. You'd have picked us *both* up floating in space. I'm never going to be like my mother."

He remembered. "You are an extraordinary female, Vivian. It's her loss."

"Thanks." She scooted closer and he opened his arms. She curled into him, letting him hold her.

He felt happy. His mate enjoyed his touch. They may never have cubs but she was more than enough. He nuzzled her head. "I should get some work in. The males have covered for me to give us time to bond. How would you like to learn what I do?"

She lifted her face to peer at him, smiling. "I'd love that! Maybe you can teach me how to do something useful around here to pull my weight."

He thought about it and understood her need to do so. "You are very useful already. You're my mate. You make me happy."

"I'm happy too. I'd still like to find something to do on your ship."

"You could make those announcements. Many males would like to learn about your females. Especially after they hear that we've mated."

"Are you going to tell them?"

He nodded. "I will register our mating with my home world. We all do. Our king will be notified, too, since I need to report what happened with your vessel. We're required to do that when we have any contact with another alien race."

"Are you sure your people are going to be okay with us?"

"Certain." He nuzzled her head again. "They will be happy for us."

"I'll stop worrying then." She uncurled from him and stood. "Show me your ship and let's find me a job."

He rose to his feet and took her hand. "Just stay close to me. That's more than enough."

He meant it. Being near Vivian and looking at her made him happy and content. Having a mate was the best thing ever.

Chapter Fourteen

Vivian typed in the last sentence and read over what she'd written. She'd chosen report format, the way the cultural center requested. It was how she was trained to assess aliens and record information. Only now she wasn't sending it back to Earth, and the topic was about human women.

The doors behind her opened and she turned, smiling at Brassi. He checked on her often when she spent time on the computer in his office. He had a small one off the common room. He held a snack and a drink.

"You've been in here for hours." He placed the plate and cup down, moving behind her to stare at the screen. "I can't read it."

"I have to translate it into your language, and then you can read it over." She looked up at him. "I'm nervous."

He leaned down and nuzzled her head. She smiled, loving that he did that often, along with giving her kisses.

There was no doubt she was already madly in love with Brassi. The words hadn't been said but they weren't needed. She knew he felt the same for her.

"How did inventory go?"

He sat on the edge of the desk. "Nothing is missing. It never is. We just do it out of habit before we land or dock to offload."

"Better to be safe than sorry. What's the cargo again?"

"We traveled to that out-of-the-way planet to buy seeds for a growing colony. That's why we were in your part of space when we heard your distress signal. This colony we're approaching asked us to gain them various samples. We have hundreds of crates of seeds."

"Did they pay you well?"

He grinned. "Yes, and I found a mate. Best trip so far."

"Yes, it was."

He glanced at her screen. "How did your announcement turn out?"

"I basically went over how we met and mated."

He frowned.

"I didn't go into many details. Just introduced myself, gave the basic rundown of us meeting, and the attraction we felt. I explained some of our physical differences and how we mated. I made it clear human women wouldn't be wrestling with your males to show sexual interest."

"I look forward to reading it."

"You can veto anything I put in there, and I'll fix it."

"Veto?"

"Change it. Take it out." She picked up what looked similar to a sushi roll and popped it into her mouth. It wasn't raw fish. Just rounded white rice-like cakes with some kind of cooked meat in the center. They seemed fried, and were very tasty. "Are you sure anyone on your planet will want to read this?"

He nodded. "Not only our planet, but our growing colonies. Every male in space will want to read it, too, and learn about your females, since we're compatible."

She grinned. "Very compatible, and often."

He chuckled. "We work."

"Yes, we do. I wish I could write something like this for Earth, to let our women know what they're missing out on, to encourage them to mate with Veslors. But we haven't heard from Abby." Her good mood faded. "So for all I know, Earth has an arrest warrant out for me. It's only been three weeks since you picked me up. The investigation may not have even started yet."

He slid off the desk and surprised her by scooping her out of the chair. She wrapped her arms around his neck. "They are stupid if they decide you did anything wrong. They won't arrest you regardless. We can avoid any Earth allies, if that's so."

"You want to open trade negotiations with United Earth."

"For my people. I won't risk you, mate. We've done great without them so far. We'll continue to do so."

"What if your king makes alliances with Earth and they order me turned over to them?"

"I told you that it won't happen. I sent in my report, and even spoke to my king."

"I know. You said he was glad that we'd mated, and I'm considered a Veslor now. Earth can put a lot of pressure on others, though. They're really good at that."

"Stop worrying." He carried her toward the door. "You need to not think."

She grinned. "You just want me naked."

"Always. Work is done. Now we bond in our quarters."

They were in the lift when nausea hit her suddenly. She wiggled. "Put me down!"

Brassi lowered her, and she put her hand over her mouth, trying to breathe through her nose and fight the urge to be sick. The lift stopped and opened. She rushed out and found a trash panel, yanking it open. She quickly lost the meager contents of her stomach.

Brassi gently held her until she was done. He snarled, rubbing her back. "That's the third time it's happened. We're going to see Vassi, *now*."

She shook her head. "No. It's just me adjusting to your food. I guess those round meat things are out. Just like that chili-like stuff I ate the other night that made me throw up. It guess it was too spicy."

"You've eaten that meat before and weren't sick. I'm taking you to Vassi."

"I'm fine, Brassi. Food adjustments. That's all. I had the same thing happen when I went to Earth at first. I wasn't used to eating that much real meat. Most of the stuff on fleet vessels are plant-based and just flavored to *taste* like meat."

He scooped her up and turned them, entering the lift again. She kept her face averted, since she figured her breath would be bad. He got off on the next level and carried her to his brother's door, chiming to get in.

It opened, and Vassi stood there in just shorts. "Meet us in medical." Brassi strode away, down the hallway to the exam room. He carried her inside and put her on the bed.

She slid off it and went to the sink, opening one of the drawers beside it until she found what she was looking for. It had been a glorious day when she'd discovered Veslors had toothbrushes and toothpaste.

Vassi kept paired packets of them in the exam room. She brushed her teeth and cleaned her mouth.

The door opened, and she turned. Vassi had put on more clothing and looked alarmed now, with worry in his eyes.

"What's wrong?"

"My mate lost the contents of her stomach again."

"It's just me adjusting to your food." She gave him a shrug. "I told Brassi I'm okay. I feel fine now."

"Up." Vassi pointed.

When she finished rinsing her mouth, Brassi grabbed her before she could move and put her back on the bed. He adjusted her as if she were a child, draping her gently over the surface. She sighed, peering up at him. "I'm *fine*. You worry too much."

"You're my mate. My heart." His voice deepened. "We don't know much about humans. What if you picked up a virus that is harmless to us, but not to you?"

"I gave her every vaccine we have," Vassi reminded him. "I uploaded all medical information available about her race to our computer. There was a lot. They don't hide that information from others." He turned on the scanner and the large machine above her lowered.

Brassi stepped back but still hovered close. "I will feel better once you check her."

"I'm doing it." Vassi met her gaze. "What does it mean when humans vomit?"

"That food didn't agree with us for some reason, or we've picked up a virus of some kind. It's only happened three times, and I always feel better right after. The last time was four days ago."

"I don't like it," Brassi growled.

"Me either. Puking isn't fun." She tried to get him to smile but he didn't, glaring at his brother instead.

"Find what's wrong with her and fix it."

Vassi nodded. "It probably is the food. What was it this time? The ket stew?"

"No. I avoided your version of chili after the last time."

The scanner started, a low hum filling the room. Vassi grabbed a pad, reading as the machine sent data to it. "Your temperature is a degree higher than normal."

"Probably from puking."

He suddenly shot his hand out and touched something on the side of the bed, his features tensing.

"What is it? Is she sick?" Brassi stepped closer.

Vassi jerked away, pressed the pad to his chest briefly, eyes widening, and then he ran his fingers over the side of the bed where the scan controls were located.

Finally, after a few tense minutes, he met Vivian's gaze. "I know what is making you sick."

"Is it curable?" Brassi grabbed Vassi by the arm. "Tell me you can fix her!"

His brother broke free of Brassi's hold. "Calm. I'm going to show you." He moved around to the other side of the bed and picked up another tablet device, tapping into it. "There's no reason for alarm." He suddenly grinned when he looked up. "Watch."

He tapped the tablet and a screen slid down from the wall next to him. It came on, and then an image filled the monitor.

Vivian stared at it, trying to make sense of what she was seeing—then she panicked, grabbing for Brassi.

But he didn't reach for her. He was staring at the screen with his mouth hanging open and his eyes wide.

She clutched his arm. "What is that?"

He didn't seem to hear her, his focus completely on the screen. She turned her head to look at it again. Whatever showed on the monitor was moving slightly.

Vassi chuckled and zoomed in on the blob...and what Vivian saw then shocked her to her core. It was a live feed of something inside a sack full of fluid. The shape became clearer—and it finally sank in.

It was a tiny alien panther curled into a ball.

"Your mate is breed compatible," Vassi announced. "There is your son! Vivian is approximately three weeks along. You did more than mate—you created life together! Your son is probably the source of her puking. It's very common with pregnancy."

Tears blinded her. She was *pregnant*?

Brassi grabbed hold of her hand on his arm, and she turned her head. He had tears in his eyes, too. His mouth closed, opened, then closed again. He stumbled closer and bent, putting his head against hers, nuzzling her.

She was pregnant! They hadn't thought it was possible. Then something occurred to her. "It looks like your battle form."

Brassi nodded against her and released her hand, wrapping his arm around her ribs, hugging her. He kept his face buried in her hair and his body shook.

Vassi moved around the bed and smiled at her, putting his hand on Brassi's back. "He's overcome with happiness. Give him a minute. Every male wants cubs, but we thought it might not be possible with humans. We were wrong...and that's a great thing."

Brassi nodded against her again and squeezed her gently. "Happy," he rasped.

She blinked back tears. "Me too. Stunned though." She reached up and caressed the back of his head but kept her attention on Vassi. "It's in battle form, right?"

"All infants are born that way."

"Wow. I didn't know that. So it's got claws? Is that safe for me?"

"The claws and sharp teeth won't present until after a cub is born. You're safe."

She felt extremely grateful for that. She'd seen Brassi shifted, and his claws were terrifyingly sharp. "How big will this baby get?"

Vassi reached out and gently touched her stomach, petting her, before picking up a pad and tapping it. "Average human baby weight is seven to eight pounds, according to what I've learned. Average Veslor cub births are between five and six pounds. What may be curious is the span of your pregnancy." He glanced up at the monitor. "I have to ask. Have you two copulated with Brassi in battle form again, since you mated?"

Brassi cleared his throat and moved, nuzzling her once more before he straightened. He took her hand, pulled it to his mouth, and kissed it. Their gazes met and he grinned. "We're having a cub."

"We are."

"I need to know. One of you answer me, please. Was it only when you mated or again since?"

Brassi answered his brother. "Why do you ask?"

"If it was just when you mated, by the rate of growth of your cub, her pregnancy is proceeding in the common Veslor way. If not, I'm alarmed by the size."

Vivian reached down to touch her stomach. "Is something wrong?" It would devastate her. She'd just found out she was pregnant! Nothing could happen to their baby. He was her and Brassi's miracle.

"Just the once, when we mated," Brassi told him.

Vivian nodded. "We've talked about doing it again but we already damaged one couch."

Vassi frowned. "How?"

"The cub," Brassi reminded him. "What does it mean? Is our son fine?"

Vassi stared at the monitor, tapped on his pad, and finally smiled at them. "He's perfectly healthy, and growing just like a Veslor."

"Because he's in that form instead of your, um, relaxed one?" Vivian was still a bit wigged out that her baby was in alien panther form instead of looking more like a combination of her and Brassi.

"His size. As I said, all our infants are born in battle form. They won't shift until after birth, when they learn to control their emotions."

She took that in, surprised by the information. She'd thought their *current* form was their natural one. Instead, it seemed alien panther was. "What about his size?"

"Human pregnancies last nine months. Which would mean your son would be much smaller than he is. Veslor pregnancies are three months. That's the size of your son as he should be at this point." Vassi put down his pad and used his hands to make a shape about the size of a baseball. "He's growing at a perfect Veslor rate."

She looked from his hands to the screen, before reaching down to her stomach. She had noticed that her belly was growing a bit but Brassi was always bringing her snacks. The male was obsessed with keeping her well-fed. She hadn't gained much weight, though. Maybe two or three pounds.

Then she replayed what Vassi had told her, did the math—and was glad she was lying down.

In just over two months, their son would be born.

Brassi moved closer and gently brushed her hand aside, resting his large palm over her belly. She met his gaze. He grinned wide. She couldn't help but feel his happiness.

"You need to eat more," Vassi explained. "Avoid fried foods and anything with cha spice. That is probably what made you vomit. It's typical with our females. I would have warned you and run a scan if I'd thought you could breed. I'm sorry, Vivian. You never should have gotten sick. It's my fault."

"No, it's not." She shook her head, unable to look away from Brassi. "We didn't think we could get pregnant."

"We were wrong," Brassi whispered, caressing her stomach tenderly. "We will have a cub. I'm the luckiest male."

"I'm going to have to make a list of questions. Please tell me that your women push out babies, and they don't, like...claw their way out."

Brassi's eyes widened, and he turned to Vassi.

Vassi chuckled. "Birthing is the same for both races. Cubs are harmless in pregnancy. As I said, he has no sharp claws now. After he's born, his claws will grow and thicken. No teeth to worry over until he's about six months old. It is also safe for you to copulate for now. I'll keep doing checkups every week and let you know if that changes." He put down his pad and nodded to his brother. "Take your mate to your quarters. Avoid fried foods and cha in what she eats. Her sickness should be over."

"Human women have morning sickness," she countered.

Vassi met her gaze. "Your body is behaving like a Veslor's right now. Everything indicates it. But if you get ill again, come to me right away."

Brassi scooped her up, being extremely gentle. "Don't tell anyone. We'll share tomorrow. Right now, I want to cuddle with my mate."

"You have my word. Congratulations to us all."

Vivian curled into his chest as Brassi carried her to their quarters. Neither spoke the entire way, until he placed her on the bed and curled around her.

"We're having a baby."

He nuzzled her. "You were enough. This cub is the best surprise."

"I know. I feel the same way. I just hope I can be a good mom to a Veslor."

"You're a perfect mate. You'll be the perfect mother."

"Do we need to buy a bigger ship?" She feared he'd say yes, and it would be a financial burden.

"No. We have storage space we can convert next door."

She sighed in relief. "Good. How do you think everyone is going to respond?"

"They will be thrilled. Everyone loves a cub."

She relaxed. "Even Nessel?"

He chuckled deeply. "He'll grumble...but you watch. He'll spoil our cub the most when he thinks no one is looking."

Epilogue

Three months later

"Vivian!"

She startled and lifted her head from the data pad she was studying. Veslor language was hard to learn, but she was doing it slowly.

Kavs rushed into the common room, out of breath.

"What's wrong?" She was on her feet in a heartbeat.

"Come to the bridge. There's an incoming message."

"From your planet?"

"For you."

She felt stunned but then rushed toward him. "From who?"

He snagged her hand and pulled her along, toward the front of the ship. She saw the others inside once they entered the bridge, including her mate. He sat behind the coms seat with their son cuddled in his sling-like carrier against his bare chest. She approached him and put her hands on his warm shoulders.

She glanced down at their sleeping cub. They'd named him Klad, after Brassi's grandfather. He was the cutest alien panther baby ever. Within a year, he'd start shifting and learn how to stay in his more human-like relaxed state. Until then, she was the mother of a cub. It didn't bother her one bit.

Brassi reached up and gripped her hand on his shoulder, and she lifted her gaze to his. His golden stare always made her feel loved. "It's Abby."

Her heart raced, and she looked at the large dark monitor. "Are you sure?"

"Yes. She's been pinging us, and I responded. She's getting a stronger signal and will call back, now that she's locked on to our location."

"How did she find us? Never mind. It's Abby. I forgot how good she is at hacking into systems."

There was a ping, and Brassi flicked a switch. The monitor came on and a pretty face appeared.

Abby sat on a couch in what looked like a large room. The big window in the background showed blue skies. Her red hair was pulled up into a bun and she wore a short green dress. A smile curved her lips.

"I found you!"

"Abby, are you on Earth?"

"Yes." She glanced over her shoulder and then peered back. "It's a beautiful day in Los Angeles. Clear skies. Not that *you* probably give a shit. I wanted to let you know that we've both been cleared. It's safe for you to come home! That dickhead Alderson and his cronies tried like hell to throw us under the bus, but I'd already started streaming video before they blew up some systems on the *Gorison Traveler* in their sad attempts to damage the computers storing all the security footage."

"Under a bus?"

Vivian ignored Ruggler's whisper. "I'm just glad you're okay. I was worried they might try to kill you, too."

"Oh, they tried." Abby flashed a smirk. "They were planning on blowing through a hull to reach me, so I locked down the blast walls around Control One. Then I hacked the entertainment rooms to broadcast footage of Commander Alderson and the idiots plotting with him, discussing how to destroy the main computers to help them shove the blame of what happened onto Big Mike, some of the other crew who died, and on you. That didn't go over so well with most of the crew. Especially when I also uploaded the security footage of those two hookers being interviewed about what Alderson had done to them during lockdown. Every woman on the ship wanted to remove the man's balls!"

"I take it that an admiral eventually arrived to get bridge access open?"

"Yes. I just got back to Earth a few days ago. I had to testify, but I'd already forwarded all the footage, so the investigation was swift and pretty much at its end when I arrived. We're in the clear. Alderson has been kicked out of the fleet. He's persona non grata now. The press is tearing him apart. Oh, and his wife filed for divorce. I saw that on the news feeds this morning. Over two dozen of the men working with him, also plotting to lie about what really happened, also got stripped of fleet clearance, and some are facing prison time."

Something caught Vivian's attention. Some kind of floating device outside. "What's that in the window behind you?"

Abby turned, cursed, and jumped up from her couch. She ran to the window and pushed a button. A shutter came down swiftly, sealing it off.

Auto-lights came on in the room as she returned to the couch and took a seat. "Damn drones. It's the press. I'm twenty-six floors up, but that doesn't matter." She sighed. "Everyone wants an interview with me. I'm refusing. It was bad enough when I had to leave my home to testify. You can't imagine how many photos they've taken of me. Fair warning—they're going to be all over *you* when you come home. You can stay with me. My penthouse has damn good security."

Vivian bit her lip. "I'm not coming back."

Abby leaned forward. "It's safe, Vivian. I had my family attorneys represent you, too. We both have immunity and were cleared of all the charges Alderson attempted to bring against us. Hell, we're heroes! They even want to throw us some kind of parade in New York. No one is going to arrest you. The worst you have to worry about are those damn reporters and their drones."

Then Abby pointed toward Brassi. "Oh, I have great news for you, too! Your king should have been contacted already, or will be soon. The Veslors are also heroes, now that everything has been revealed. A lot of people are very interested in working with your people, especially when a little digging proved you guys are high in food supplies with the trading you do." She grinned. "I sent a personal message to your king today, giving him the advice to play hardball with whomever contacts him. Food supplies are gold to some of the colonies."

Brassi frowned.

"That's good," Vivian whispered. "I'll explain it later."

He relaxed in his seat.

Vivian was relieved that she wasn't a criminal, and that the Veslors might get some good trade agreements from United Earth. She leaned forward and reached over her mate, gently lifting their son from the pouch Brassi wore on his chest. Abby wouldn't have been able to see him otherwise.

She cuddled their cub to her chest, and then stepped forward, closer to the screen, twisting her body to show his sleeping face to her friend.

Abby's mouth dropped open.

"Meet Klad. Brassi and I mated, and had a baby."

Abby seemed speechless.

"My life is now on the *Brar*, and I'm extremely happy. Thank you for clearing my name and letting me know I'm not a criminal on the run...but Earth isn't in my future."

"He's so damn cute!" Abby slid off the couch to her knees, getting closer to the monitor. Her friend met her gaze, then glanced at Brassi before looking back at her. Abby smirked again. "I guess you let him *comfort* you more. Good for you."

Brassi pulled Vivian onto his lap. "Good for *me*."

Abby laughed. "This is the best news ever. You got your sexy, hot alien and his baby. I envy you."

Kavs suddenly rushed forward. "I'm looking for a mate." He whipped off his shirt. "I'd love to comfort you, female." Then he opened his arms. "I'm here waiting for you if you wish to fly to us. I would be eager to try to have a cub with you."

Abby stared hard at the male, mouth agape, and finally smiled. "You're a charmer...and nice chest. *Really* nice chest. I'm stuck here for a while though. The family is a bit upset with me after I made hacking our systems look so easy. It wasn't, actually, but public opinion and all that." Abby paused then shook her head. "Put your shirt back on, hot stuff. You're distracting me."

Kavs put his shirt on. "She called me hot stuff. Is that good?"

"Yes." Vivian rolled her eyes. "I told you all that you're attractive to human females. There's your proof." She shrugged at Abby. "Brassi and I are the only mated couple on the ship. Five single guys. Know any single ladies?"

Abby opened her mouth then closed it. She shook her head. "Not any that I think would be good enough for them. My family runs in the wrong circles, if you know what I mean. I wouldn't wish a spoiled debutant on any hot alien guy. I'll keep my eye open, though, and send a message if I find someone I think would be a good fit." She winked. "Someone like you."

A buzzer sounded on Abby's end, and her expression hardened. "Shit. More press. They must've bypassed security. It's a circus here." She stared into the camera. "I have to go, but I'll call you soon. I encoded my direct number. It's for my travel device. You can reach me wherever I go on Earth—and if I ever flee this mess when my parents feel we've handled the fallout from what happened on the *Gorison Traveler*."

Abby stared at Kavs for a few long seconds.

"So damn tempting." She waved. "Take care—and congratulations. I want pictures of Klad, and think of me if your son needs a godmother. I'd be thrilled!"

The coms ended.

Vivian leaned into Brassi and smiled up at him. "I'm not a criminal."

"You never were." He cuddled her closer on his lap and nuzzled her head, petting their sleeping son's back.

"Do you think that female will come here for me?"

Vivian smiled and ignored Kavs. Most of the single males on their ship were highly interested in mating to a human, now that she'd had Brassi's cub. Nessel was the only one who denied wanting one. He didn't sound too convincing to Vivian though.

"We should celebrate." Brassi tightened his hold on her and stood.

She never worried about him dropping her, even when she was carrying their son. Her mate was really strong.

"Give me Klad," Vassi offered. "You can copulate without distraction."

"No, give me the cub," Yoniv protested. "It's my turn."

"Mine," Ruggler snarled. "You held him this morning."

"So did you," Kavs threw in. "It's *my* turn."

Brassi stopped by the door and sighed, looking down at her. "They need more cubs to share."

She laughed. "Hey, Nessel?"

The male rushed to her, and Vivian offered her son to him. He grinned widely, gently taking the cub in his arms. He never asked to hold him, but she knew he was just as fond of their son as the others.

He fled the bridge with the baby.

"That's not fair," Ruggler growled.

"Why him?" Yoniv sounded pissed.

"He's my brother's cub." Vassi pouted.

Vivian wrapped her arms around Brassi's neck. "Run, before they start wrestling."

He chuckled and took off toward their quarters, moving fast.

They passed Nessel, who was humming to their son. He might be a grump, but he loved their cub.

They reached their quarters and Brassi placed her on her feet. "We need more cubs just to keep the peace."

She laughed, taking off her clothes. "You just want another baby."

"I do. I want many cubs with you."

"I want everything with you."

Brassi stripped naked and opened his arms. "This is how it began, and this is always how it will be. I offer all that I am to you."

She walked into his arms and loved when they closed around her, holding her tight. "We need a breeding bench, since we replaced the damaged couch. I don't want to tear up another one."

He nuzzled her head. "I ordered one after Klad was born. We pick it up on our next stop."

She lifted her head. "Seriously?"

He nodded, a sexy gleam in his eye. "I had hope that you'd want more cubs."

She slid her hands to his face and pulled him down. He lowered, and she went up on her tiptoes, kissing him. They were going to try for another cub. She couldn't wait to see what a breeding bench looked like—and how much fun it would be to use it.

Life with a Veslor mate was the best thing ever.

About the Author

NY Times and USA Today Bestselling Author

I'm a full-time wife, mother, and author. I've been lucky enough to have spent over two decades with the love of my life and look forward to many, many more years with Mr. Laurann. I'm addicted to iced coffee, the occasional candy bar (or two), and trying to get at least five hours of sleep at night.

I love to write all kinds of stories. I think the best part about writing is the fact that real life is always uncertain, always tossing things at us that we have no control over, but when writing you can make sure there's always a happy ending. I love that about being an author. My favorite part is when I sit down at my computer desk, put on my headphones to listen to loud music to block out everything around me, so I can create worlds in front of me.

For the most up to date information, please visit my website. www.LaurannDohner.com

Made in the USA
Lexington, KY
04 May 2019